I0537479

She's Marrying My Man

Dominique Lewis

For Dominique

I've stared at this line over and over again in an Eric Jerome Dickey book and it inspired and pushed me to continue writing. There's countless names I could place here, but for the first book, I choose me. It took over eight years to step out in faith so proving to *myself* --my biggest critic-- that I can do it!

Enjoy!

CHAPTER 1

"Please tell me this is a nightmare."

Laila placed her hand to her head as it slowly began to throb.

"Laila, it's right here in plain English," Kecia showed her best friend their local newspaper and read, "Melanie Elle Taylor and Quinton Davon Harris will unite as one on April 22 at 2:00p.m."

"In two weeks!" Laila said in shock.

"Hold on, let me see that," their friend, Gia grabbed the newspaper, "She's really marrying your man."

"High school infatuation," Laila corrected her. Gia laid the paper on the table in front of Laila.

As Laila looked at their picture, it finally hit her; the woman she trusted and forgave repeatedly since the eighth grade was about to marry the man who had been her dream man since she was twelve-years-old. She kept staring at the black and white photo. Melanie and Quinton looked like the perfect couple who were deeply in love.

Suddenly, tears slowly filled Laila's eyes; her vision became blurry and the world seemed surreal. Laila's heart pounded rapidly, and her mind filled to the rim with confusion. They were sitting on her lanai, having an intimate barbecue at her new home in a small town in Georgia, near Atlanta called Layville. It was supposed to be a sunny day. A day that she and her two closest friends could enjoy, but a rain cloud covered them and brought coldness to Laila's heart.

Birds were chirping a sweet, sad song. One of her neighbors was mowing the lawn. The smoky aroma from the grill tickled her nostrils, and her stomach mumbled invariable complaints, but how could she eat knowing that one of her best friends was about to marry her "unofficial" high school sweetheart. Gia and Kecia had always thought of Melanie as a frenemy, but Laila had continually given her the benefit of the doubt.

Gia arose from one of the cherry oak patio chairs and walked across the beige and brown marble flooring. Gia and Kecia were still talking, but Laila's mind refused to decipher their words. She kept looking around her own yard to take her mind off the wretched news she had just received. Houses surrounded her home, so there was little room for privacy. She had placed privacy fences around the sides of the house and her backyard. Beyond the back privacy fence was a thicket of bushes near the main highway. Laila observed her landscape and noticed the flowers she had planted were starting to bloom, beautiful Fuchsias. She smiled, and then those very flowers reminded her of Quinton and brought all of her anger and hurt back to the surface.

"I can't believe this bitch didn't tell us," Gia said.

"Laila, when was the last time you talked to her?"

Laila was breathing heavily. "Uh, I don't know. I think last week some time."

"Yeah, that's when we talked to her too."

"Yeah, Kecia added me to the call," Gia added, "cuz you know I ain't bout to call the bitch. I ain't got *nothin'* to say to her."

"I just don't get it. The most clueless, naïve, and ignorant of us all was cunning enough to pull this off?" Kecia stated.

"I know right. She *never* knows what be going on, just

be in her own world. Now, we're the ones left out in the cold."

Kecia sighed. "How long do you think they've been together?"

"With Melanie, it ain't no telling," Gia said.

Laila poured another glass of wine, but this time she filled it close to the rim.

"I'm about to get another Alizé out of my cooler, any of you want one?"

"Naw, I'm still enjoying this glass of wine from Laila's collection."

"Yeah, bring me one," Laila said.

"What?"

"Ms. *Bougié* wants an Alizé?" Gia raised her brows, "Okay."

Laila hated when her friends called her bourgeois, but she had always ignored them. She didn't understand why not having a Southern accent or not using dialect made her seem uppity. Gia and Kecia enjoyed slaying the English language, even though Kecia was ironically an English teacher. Her outspoken friends even caused her to slip every once in a while. She typically brushed their comments off. However, this particular day, she was not feeling like herself. "Gia, I'm not in my right mind right now. Don't have me to get ghetto on your ass."

"Too late," Kecia snickered at her failed attempt to be firm with Gia.

Gia held her hands up. "Hey, I don't wanna start anything. I feel your pain. I knew exactly how you felt about Quinton in high school."

"*Tsk*, we all knew," Kecia agreed, rolling her eyes. Then, she placed her hand on Laila's hand and looked her in the eye, "And we all know that you still have feelings for him."

"No, I don't."

"A lie! Girl, just the other day, you were going through my yearbook talking about you should have gotten with that," Gia said.

"No, I didn't."

"But you were thinking it,"

"Laila, it is plain to see you still have feelings for the man, you just built a home only a few blocks from his mother's house," Kecia added.

"Yeah, you know that momma's boy gon' always come down and visit his momma."

"No, I didn't have him in mind when I picked this location. This is a nice neighborhood. Besides, I thought Quinton was living in Paris, not with Melanie."

They looked at her strangely.

"Well, obviously, he's been right *on top* of our so-called best friend in the States."

Laila cut her eyes at Gia. Those words pierced her soul.

Gia held up her hands again. "Hey, I'm just saying." Her signature words.

It hurt Laila to think of Quinton actually having sex with Melanie, when she had wanted him for all of these years, hoping that one day they would cross paths again. Then, they could finally have a second chance at love. She could finally give her mind, body, heart, and soul to him, but her back-stabbing, heartless, deceitful friend beat her to the punch.

She should have literally punched me in the face and stabbed me in the back herself. Maybe it wouldn't hurt as much.

Gia, guzzling her Alizé, sat adjacent from Laila. She was beautiful. Caramel brown complexion. High cheekbones. Brown eyes. She was a tall, slender woman. She started on their high school basketball team during her junior and senior year. Though most of her old teammates had let time loosen their waistbands, Gia still maintained her slender physique. She had always been a B-cup, but had enough junk in her trunk to make every man – especially when she wore her signature black mini or blue jean booty shorts – turn their heads twice. She swung her long shimmering hair behind her shoulders so it would hang down her back. Her hair was a natural black hue and always silky like she had just gotten a fresh perm. She had an oval face with a beautiful clear complexion. She barely wore makeup, but she always made sure her brows were arched and her lips were dressed in clear gloss. She had always looked like the girl-next-door, but her sharp tongue and Southern dialect revealed her true demeanor.

Gia stared at Quinton and Melanie's picture.

"This bitch got some explaining to do," she got up once again, "I think you gon' need some Rosé too."

"Now, you know she doesn't need all of that alcohol. Remember when Fluffy died. She drank almost every day."

Laila rolled her eyes. She was over losing her white terrier, Fluffy. Fluffy was the only family she had left, but once she saw that Kecia and Gia would always be there for her, she realized that she always had a family, her girls. She was living in Atlanta, but moved back to her hometown so she could be close to them.

Gia sat Laila's bottle of Rosé by the original Alizé. She opened both bottles for her sad friend. Laila just stared at the bottles; she had no intention on drinking the red and pink beverages. She rested her elbow on the glass table and laid her face upon her hand. One tear fell as she stared at her reflection. She had changed a lot since her early high school years from big glasses, flowered shirts, light blue jeans, and frizzy curly hair (that was always pulled into a ponytail) to a beautiful stylish woman. Laila was light-skinned with an oval face, high cheekbones, cinnamon brown eyes, a small pointy nose, rosy plump lips, and curly black hair worn at shoulder length. She sighed.

Kecia studied the paper again. "Wait a minute. Hold the hell on."

"What is it girl?" Gia was over at the grill once again.

"It says right here that Quinton and Melanie both graduated from Tennessee State University."

"What?" Laila couldn't believe what she was hearing. "No, no. That must be a typo because Melanie went to the

W." For years, Melanie had convinced Laila that she was attending a college in Mississippi.

"Well, honey. That w-h-o-r-e," Gia said rolling her eyes, twisting her head, and rolling her neck, "must have ventured further north during her senior year."

"Yeah, you know we didn't see her that year or the year after. We barely even talked to her, and she never invited us to her graduation."

"And where does she live now?"

"Tennessee."

"Exactly."

She had managed to keep up with Quinton. She knew that he had first went to a community college and received an associate's degree in Graphic Design. She knew he went into Marketing at TSU and that he didn't come home during school breaks, only for four holidays: Thanksgiving, Christmas, Mother's Day and Fourth of July.

"But I just don't understand. I thought Quinton was in Paris," Laila repeated again. She had remembered overhearing his aunt telling the greeter, Ms. Helen at Wal-Mart about Quinton receiving an opportunity with an agency in France, "The dates just don't add up."

"Well honey, from this wedding announcement, it's obvious that they're both in town."

"And Lucy got some 'splaining' to do," Gia attempted to mimic Ricky Ricardo, but actually sounded like a Latino woman from Brooklyn.

Lucy. That was Melanie's legal middle name that she despised in high school. They called her Lucy just to get under her skin, so they could see her turn beet red. Apparently, she changed her name from Melanie Lucy Taylor to Melanie Elle Taylor.

Gia sighed.

"That *b* always wanted what you got. I remember when she wore the same dress as you to *both* of our proms, tryna be like you,"

Kecia gasped. "She sho'll did! Except hers were white."

6

"Ol' wannabe LisaRaye ass," Gia said clanging her tongs, "And she don' went and stole the only man Laila's ever loved. Ugh,"

Laila blew her breath. "Well, there's no need for me to be angry," she interlocked her fingers, "I don't have feelings for Quinton anymore."

"Whatever you say, Laila," Kecia said. Gia sat the plate of food in the center of the table. Grilled Chicken. Burgers. Barbecued ribs. Grilled Corn.

"Hey, I'm about to get me some baked beans and potato salad, you want any?"

"No, just get me the gallon of Cherry Garcia out of the fridge."

Laila had always saved ice cream for a rainy day. Though there was not a cloud in the sky, there was still that rain cloud over her heart. She needed some comfort, and Ben and Jerry were the only two men who could appease her.

Gia and Kecia were in the kitchen, dipping spoons into the homemade dishes they had brought to the barbecue. Laila stared at the plate that lay before her. Just to think, at one point, she was pondering the thought of becoming a vegetarian, but she just had to have some meat whether it was just chicken or shrimp. The aroma of Gia and Kecia's smoked barbecue ribs and hamburgers made her skinless char-grilled chicken breast and corn look as appetizing as a cardboard box.

Kecia's rib that she staked her claim on earlier was calling Laila's name. In a matter of seconds, she discovered a new comfort. She reached for the rib, but quickly pulled her hand back. Then she grabbed it, *Ouch! Hot!* With fingers drenched in sauce, she blew, and then tore into it, cooling it in her mouth as she chewed. The burst of juices, spices, and texture made her forget about any lies and betrayal.

Gia and Kecia were laughing about something that happened at Gia's beauty salon, and then stopped in their tracks.

"Ms. Health Guru is eating on some barbecued ribs?"

"Hold up! Is that my piece?" Kecia sighed, "Well, I'm supposed to be on a diet anyway. I guess I wasn't meant to eat it." Laila could never understand why Kecia dieted. She was a very beautiful plus-sized woman. She had a milk chocolate skin tone, dark brown eyes, full lips, and always wore her long jet black hair curled. She would go on different diets and complain that she would only lose fat in her face and nowhere else.

"Uh, uh, uh," Gia shook her head, "Look at this hefa."

"Laila, sweetie," Kecia called in an effort to get her attention. She was eating like she was starving. She was almost down to the gristle when she finally realized her girls, with their meatless plates in their hands, staring at her in the doorway.

She dropped the remnants in her plate. She looked innocent and shrugged, "Sorry, Kecia."

She grabbed the bottle of Alizé, and guzzled it like a pro - like Gia. Purple was joined by red, and now more red. Wine, Meat, and Alizé. *I wish I can turn Melanie purple and red.*

"Wow."

"Now, she's going to be sick."

"She gon' say to us, 'I only eat healthy foods. Maybe a pizza or ice cream every now and then, and a sip of alcohol at night.' A lie."

"That's right, I forgot the ice cream," Kecia said as they sat down.

"I'm sorry. I grew hungry all of a sudden."

"Sure you did," Gia grabbed a burger and a piece of grilled chicken while Kecia grabbed a burger.

"I'm going to let you slide from eating my food, but it's plain to see that you have a problem with those two being together."

"No, the problem I have is her not telling me."

"Yeah, ain't no telling how many years that bitch been

lying to us. Then, to add insult to injury, she steals yet another one of Laila's men."

"I forgot about that. She stole Wesley from me in the 10th grade!" Laila had a crush on an 11th grader, Wesley Green for about a month, and Melanie quickly got involved with him. Then, Laila focused back on her obsession with Quinton.

"Yeah, she's always had some sort of demented idolization of you," Gia said, then took a bite of chicken. Kecia and Laila quickly looked at Gia. "What?"

Gia had her moments of speaking very intelligently, and then she would revert back to words like swaggtastic, gucci, and her favorite, conversate.

"She would visit me in Buckhead all of the time, and I would go up to see her. But never did she mention Quinton. Not even last Christmas. I saw no pictures. She told me she was with someone named," she looked up at the sky trying to remember the name, then frowned, "Uh, I'm so stupid."

"What?"

"Davon,"

"As in Quinton Davon Harris," Gia said.

Kecia shook her head. "That sneaky bitch."

"Vindictive, indeed," Laila nodded.

Gia started smacking, "Um, this grilled chicken is good. Kecia pass me that corn-on-the-cob."

"Here girl," Kecia handed her the entire plate, "Instead of talking about her, we need to hear what this hefa has to say." She wiped her hand with a moist towelette.

"She's just wrong. Been wrong all of her life," she said as she took a bite of corn.

Kecia pulled her cell out of her purse. "I'm gonna get to the bottom of this," she said as she dialed, and then placed the call on speaker mode. Classical music began playing.

Gia looked up. "What the hell? We callin' a bill collector or something?"

Kecia snickered, "Shut up, girl."

Then, they finally heard Melanie's light cheery voice, "Good day, Melanie Taylor speaking."

"It's messed up how we had to hear your business in the damn streets."

"Pardon me? May I ask who's speaking?"

"Oh, so she don't know us now," Gia snapped.

"Who do you think this is?"

"Oh, Kecia," she laughed uneasily, "I'm sorry; I have a new phone and I haven't pro-" "Quit lying" Gia said.

"Gia?"

"All day, every day."

"Hi, where are you two? I just came from your apartment, Kecia, and you weren't there."

"So you're in town?" Kecia asked.

"Yes, I thought I might surprise you girls."

"Yeah, we were surprised alright," Gia and Kecia said simultaneously. Laila shook her head. They were like two peas in a pod like Melanie and her once were. Little did she know, they would share everything.

Melanie repeated, "Where are you two?"

"We're with Laila, on her patio."

"Well, that is great because I'm right outside." They heard her car horn beep. The girls looked at Laila and at that moment, her heart and mind were racing at 100 miles per hour, one trying to beat the other, and she's praying to God they don't crash. *Please slow down, so I can keep my composure.*

"Well, the front door is open." Kecia ended the call.

Laila held her head with one hand and her chest with the other for a moment until she calmed down. Even though Melanie was only a few feet away, she just couldn't bear the thought of looking at her. Laila observed Gia and Kecia's disgusted faces and realized what they were about to say to Melanie.

"Girls, whatever you do," she looked directly at Kecia, "Please don't fuss at her for being with Quinton. I don't want her thinking I still have feelings for him after all these years."

"But you do!" They both said in frustration as if they were desperately trying to bring their friend back from a world of denial. The ladies could never understand Laila's unending obsession with Quinton. It was a fascination and love they never understood and seemingly never will especially since Quinton had never exhibited the same feelings, not even a fraction of it; at least Gia and Kecia hadn't seen it.

Laila quickly grabbed a moist towelette and wiped her mouth and hands to erase any trace of barbecue sauce. Then she rubbed the traces of grease that she had unknowingly placed on her chest. Gia was staring at her.

"That's right. I forgot the Queen of Bougie is on her way. Kecia, I got any meat or corn in my teeth? I don't want this bitch picking out any flaws even though I *know* I'm flawless." She grinned.

"No girl. You're good. Am I?" Kecia grinned.

"Yeah girl."

"Laila?" She showed them her teeth.

"Girl, you got barbecue sauce all on the right side of your face."

"Really?" She quickly rubbed her face.

"Well alright. Now, bring this bitch on." Gia could see her approaching.

"Hey girls," Melanie appeared at the glass doors and stepped onto the marble floors of Laila's lanai.

As soon as Melanie locked eyes with them, she displayed her genuine smile. She had always been beautiful. Light Complexion. Medium length brown hair. Her hair was now enhanced with honey blonde highlights which complemented her honey brown eyes. She wore a pink quarter length sleeve blouse and white pants. It was typical; white had always been her favorite color.

Kecia got up and hugged her, "It's been a long time since I've seen you, Kecia."

"It sure has."

"And Gia," she said as Gia reluctantly got up and hugged her, "You're so beautiful."

"Um huh, I know."

"And Laila!" she hugged Laila while she was still seated.

"You have such a beautiful home. Did you have an interior designer to deck the place out?"

She gave a fake smile. "No, all me."

"And the patio flooring! I have never seen anything like it. Your house is so luxurious and elegant with a hint of oriental in its theme. I really like your Feng Shui."

Blah. Blah. Blah, Gia mouthed. Laila could tell Gia was thinking, *she ain't doing nothing but kissing ass.*

"Yes, I have to pay homage to my Asian roots."

Gia turned to Laila and pursed her lips, "Girl, you know you ain't mixed with Asian, you mixed with white."

Kecia hit Gia's leg.

"Um, what smells so good?" Melanie looked at the center of the table.

Kecia answered, "Well, as you can see. We were having a barbecue."

"Yeah, an *intimate* barbecue," Gia added.

"We have ribs, burgers, baked beans, and potato salad. You want any?"

"Oh no, I'm trying to watch my figure."

"Hmm…it figures," Gia smirked.

"Well, don't just stand there. Have a seat," Kecia gestured towards the empty chair next to Laila. She obeyed. The girls just stared at her, so Laila decided to break the ice. Even though she tried to ask her about any other topic, she blurted, "So you're marrying Quinton?"

"Yeah, how did that happen?" Gia said.

"Yes, inquiring minds would love to know," Kecia said. "Let's jump right in. Why don't we?"

None of her friends blinked as they awaited her answer.

She sighed, closed her eyes, and took a deep breath. She opened her eyes and gazed at them, blinking periodically. She always made those routine gestures when she was coming up with a plausible explanation; in other words, a good lie.

"Quinton and I discovered we lived in the same apartment complex in Tennessee. Then, we began seeing each other and things just happened from there."

You've been secretly dating the man of my dreams, and now you're about to get married and you couldn't even tell us the entire truth.

"But you two went to the same college. What about those lies?"

"And the one you're telling now."

"I am not lying. I was behind everyone one year, so I transferred to Tennessee State *after* Quinton had graduated. I was just ashamed to be behind. That's why I didn't tell you anything. Quinton and I really didn't meet up until recently at my apartment complex." The entire time, she did not blink once. That was yet another lie.

"So how long have you two been together?"

"Two years."

"Damn!" Gia exclaimed.

That's not recent!

"Two years, Melanie?" Kecia asked in disbelief.

"So you neglected to tell us you were going with her man for two years!" Gia exclaimed.

Laila's eyes bucked. "Gia!"

Melanie sighed. "I didn't tell you because I knew you would react like this. Laila, I remember how much you adored him in high school. I didn't know where your feelings stood as an adult, so I was just afraid to tell you. I really didn't think we were going to stay together that long much less get married."

Gia smirked, "Well, you haven't sealed the deal just yet."

Kecia quickly spoke up. "So why didn't you tell Laila or any of us when you realized it was much more than friendship?"

"I don't know. Still afraid, I guess. I didn't want you girls looking down on me thinking I stole Laila's man."

"Uhh huh." Gia said.

"I just preferred to face the music once I finally came home for the ceremony."

Gia frowned and mouthed, *face the music?*

Laila leaned forward. "Well, I *am* upset. Why would you think I could ever be mad at you? Girl, I don't like Quinton anymore."

Kecia and Gia looked at her in disbelief.

"Really?" Melanie's eyes brightened.

"It was a high school crush that stayed in high school, and let's be clear ladies, he was never my man. Not then and definitely not now."

"So, no hard feelings?"

"Girl no," Laila said with a fake smile.

"That's great!" Melanie jumped up and hugged her. "Well, Kecia. Gia. I would love for you girls to be my bridesmaids."

The ladies' mouths dropped and Gia frowned as she quickly turned back to Laila.

"And Laila," she held her timid friend's hands, "I would really love it if you'd be my maid of honor."

CHAPTER 2

"Mom, you know you can change my room any time you want, right?"

"Oh, you're saying that *now* since you're getting married."

Quinton was at his childhood home speaking to the mother he's always loved, honored, and adored. He was sitting on his old bed while she was standing in the doorway. The house smelled of apple pie and cinnamon.

"No, I was just thinking. You could turn this into a guest room, an office...you can even set up that sewing room you've always wanted."

"Well, I don't need more than two guest rooms. My office is just fine in the corner of my bedroom, and since I have a career, I have no time for hobbies."

"Yes ma'am, I understand."

"I'm keeping this room just the way it is, so I will always have a piece of my baby here with me. So you will know that no matter where you go in life you can always come home."

"Aw mom, you're gonna make a grown man cry."

"I'm just glad you're back from overseas. You had me worried to death."

"Mom, I was in Paris. You're acting like I was fighting the War in Iraq."

"Naw, but I was in a war with that little French hefa you were with. What was her name? Oh yeah, Genevieve. Trying to keep you from talking to me."

"Yeah, she was excessively controlling. Woo," he let out a sigh of relief to be out of that relationship, "I have only one momma, and she's right here," he got up and hugged her.

"Yes, and I only have one baby boy," she kissed him on the cheek and he sat back on his bed. His mother straightened her leopard print blouse and adjusted the charms on her bracelet. "Okay Quinton, I'm going to ask you this one time and one time only. Are you sure you're ready for marriage and are you sure you want to marry *this* girl?"

"Yes, I wouldn't have popped the question if I wasn't ready."

"Okay, just asking," she held up her hands. "You see, you can go all over the world, but you will find that the one for you has been right under your nose the entire time. I met your father in California and he followed me down here. I'm glad he gave me you, but he wasn't the one for me. When we divorced, I didn't even bother finding someone new. Now, Gary has worked with me for seven years and never did I imagine I would fall in love with him. He finally worked up the nerve to ask me on a date and we've been inseparable ever since," he saw his mother light up as she thought of him.

"Yeah, well he better be treating you right. So, when is he coming over?"

"I don't know. Right now, my main concern is your wedding."

She walked down the hall.

"Baby, your apple pie and vanilla ice cream is waiting for you when you're ready," she called.

"Okay."

"And I got the other ice cream you like, in case you want to eat some of that while you're here too. It's Cherry Garcia, right?"

"Yeah, that's it. Thanks Mom."

Quinton looked around his room. He felt a sense of nostalgia as he looked at his basketball memorabilia--a replica of his blue and gold high school jersey (jersey number 02), his basketball, and endless athletic trophies and awards. He looked at a framed picture of him and his best friend, Alonzo, in their high school days.

"That damn Alonzo," he laughed to himself. He let out a deep breath and sat at the head of his bed.

He opened the top drawer of his night stand. Then, he closed it and opened the bottom drawer, he picked up a hunter green plastic film envelope and pulled out the pictures. The first one was a picture of Laila and himself, as teens, laying on his bed. There was another picture of him and her kissing. There was yet another picture he took of her outside--a close-up of her wearing a white tank top and holding a fuchsia.

His mother appeared in the doorway once again. "You still want to have the bachelor party here?"

"Yes ma'am, if I'm not asking too much."

"No, it's fine. I just don't want a stripper bouncing her nasty ass on my bed or in my room altogether."

Quinton almost laughed at his mother's choice words. She barely used profanity unless she felt she needed to make a point.

"Mom, you know I wouldn't disrespect you like that," he smiled at her. "Besides, I don't think there's going to be any strippers."

"Is Alonzo throwing the party?"

"Yes ma'am."

"Well, there will be strippers then. Just keep in mind what I said."

CHAPTER 3

She sashayed into my house and had the audacity to ask me to be her maid of honor.

What did I do? Punch her? Curse at her? Throw her out of my home? No, I politely smiled and accepted. I know it sounds idiotic, but I didn't want her to think I still had feelings for him after all of these years. He was my high school crush, the person I could never get. Now, she has him.

Laila shook her head. Kecia was on her cell phone and stepped away from the table. Melanie watched Gia guzzle down another bottle.

"Alizé. How cliché."

Laila quickly looked at Gia, but she was in her own world. It was typical. Melanie would always throw in her insults when she knew no one was paying her any mind. She also loved to insult someone by making it seem as a compliment. If only Gia heard her…if only Kecia wasn't on the phone, they would quickly jump down her throat. Of all people, the most deceitful person on her property had the nerve to insult someone.

Kecia joined them once again with a look of worry on her face. Laila knew she was trying to get in touch with her undeserving, unappreciative boyfriend, Leonard. Just

18

weeks ago, the ladies were having a Girls' Day Out at the mall when they saw him walking with another woman. She confronted him, but he introduced the other woman as his "cousin" and made up some elaborate explanation. Kecia believed every word. Since that day, he's been spotted around town in one of his company's cars with her on the passenger's side. He may have convinced Kecia that his cousin needed his help since her husband divorced her and took everything, but Laila, Gia, and everyone else knew better.

"Laila, you're deep in thought," Melanie said.

"Oh, just thinking of what I'm going to wear to wor-"

"Your grill looks very nice," she cut her off.

"Oh, my Kenmore? I won that in a raffle at Kecia's church."

"She sho'll did. That grill is worth over $1,500. I was tryna to get Kecia to stuff the box for me," Gia said.

Kecia was busy texting. "Yep, everybody wanted that grill. I think we ended up raising over $20,000, and Laila purchased one ticket at the last minute and they pulled her name the next day."

"Wow, Laila. You've always been lucky."

"I guess I have." *Lucky in everything, but love.*

"Well, I'm sorry to cut our evening short, but uh . . . *Momma* gotsta wake up early in the morning," she said referring to herself, "so I'ma fix me a plate and be out."

"Yeah, me too. I should get going," Kecia said looking at her screen again.

Laila could tell she wanted to hurry back home to check on Leonard.

"Aw, I hate you girls have to leave," Melanie said sounding sad.

Gia and Kecia picked up all of the plates on the table.

"Yeah, well talk to ya later," Gia gave a fake smile, hurried through the glass door opening, and stood in the dining room.

"Yeah, I'll call you girls later." Kecia said looking

directly at Laila. She nodded back.

"You girls be careful," Melanie told her, "And don't forget we're having our engagement party Tuesday. I'll let you know the details."

Gia threw her hand up as she followed Kecia into the kitchen.

Melanie turned to Laila, "Now, we can have some time together and catch up."

"Oh, goodie," Laila said sarcastically with a forced smile, "Would you like some wine?" She grabbed her glass and poured as Melanie happily talked about *Blah, Blah, Blah*.

***

Kecia slowly entered her apartment. Her boyfriend, Leonard, a light-skinned, clean cut, uptight, penny loafer-wearing man, was sitting on the couch reading the newspaper while the television was on CNN.

"Hi honey." She walked behind the couch and attempted to kiss his cheek, but he pulled away.

"Where have you been?"

"Oh, with the girls." She walked over to her cherry oak dining table. "Then, afterwards, I went to the grocery store."

"So what were you doing with *the girls*?" she took items out of her bags and placed them on the table. He did not budge to help her.

"Just hanging out," she said as he got up and walked towards her. "Oh yeah, let me tell you… Melanie-"

"So what did you eat today?"

"Oh you know… some rice cakes and uh . . . a veggie burger."

He glared at her and finally said, "A veggie burger, eh?"

"Yes."

He let out a breath of frustration.

"Then, why do I smell barbecue on your breath?"

"Oh that?" she looked at him, "Uh, see what had happened was . . . I had dipped the veggie burger in the sauce, so that … that's why you-"

"I don't want to hear it! You promised me you were going to go on a diet."

"I tried to but-"

"But nothing!" he paced around, "I don't think I can be with someone who keeps lying to me."

"At least I'm not cheating on you or riding someone around in my car saying he's my cousin."

"Kecia, I told you. Tacara *is* my cousin, you can ask my mother."

"Oh, that will solve everything," she said sarcastically, "I'll just fly to London and find a mother who refuses to talk to her own son."

Then, she mumbled to herself, "I can't even find Laila's parents, so how in the hell can *I* find Ohsaree Thurman?"

He frowned. "Why are we changing the subject? We were discussing you and your diet."

"How about this? You let me worry about my diet, and I'll let you worry about your *cousin*."

"I don't see how that's a fair trade because she's really my cousin," he said with his hands on his waist. "I'm not cheating on you," he pointed his finger at her, "but you cheated on your diet and lied to me about it."

She sighed, "You're right, Leonard; it *is* time to change the subject." Everything grew quiet; she took a deep breath and smiled.

"Guess what?" she happily said. He didn't bother to respond, "My friend, Melanie is getting married and she asked me to be her bridesmaid, but the man she's-"

He smirked, "A bridesmaid, eh? I wonder how she's going to find a dress that's big enough for you." He walked down the hall and Kecia looked in utter amazement. Her eyes watered, but she held in her tears.

CHAPTER 4

Dear Journal,

I know it has been ages since I've written you. I think the last time I created an entry was when my parents decided they both did not want to claim their adult child as their daughter anymore only because of their foolish actions. I've learned to let that issue go, but Journal, my life just keeps getting better. Melanie called me last night and asked me to meet her and her "fiancé" at the bridal shop, so she can find the perfect dress. I hate I got myself into this predicament. Why did I agree to be the maid of honor? Although I try to deny it, I still have feelings for Quinton.

When I first met Quinton, I fell in love with one look into his beautiful dark brown eyes. The way he licked his lips put me in a whole world of desires. I knew he was the one, but I was afraid to take a chance on love and I missed out on possibly a lifetime of happiness. I will always regret ignoring love, ignoring my feelings, and I will always regret being the scared, safe "little girl" that I still am. Being safe has never benefited me. I've never found the one for being safe.

I honestly don't know if Quinton is the one. If he's not, then I probably have missed out on my soul mate just for being "Little Miss Perfect Laila" as everyone has always called me yet this "perfect Laila" does have flaws. I'm longing to be with and lusting after my best friend's fiancé. It sounds cruel, but he was my crush, my dream. Now he's her dream come true, and right now, I'm suffering through this nightmare. The person I've always wanted more than anyone in this world is marrying the girl I've known since I was twelve. It hurts because she knew every single feeling I had for him. I told her everything; little did I know, she felt the same way. You always want what you can't have. Indeed, a true statement.

> *Sincerely,*
> *Laila*

After writing in her journal, Laila woke up the next morning with a new perspective. She remembered that she and Melanie had gone through some rough times together. She would always love her friend. She couldn't be mad at her over a man, even if he was the man she had always wanted. A man comes a dime a dozen, but true friendship is hard to find. Even though they've had plenty of arguments in the past that Melanie typically won, Laila refused to let this fatal blow get her down.

Laila acknowledged the fact that he was never her man to begin with and Melanie wasn't alone. Quinton knew about the girls' friendship, and for him to get involved with Melanie, just allowed Laila to see that he had no interest in reuniting with her in the first place. Laila got ready to meet the happy couple at the bridal shop. She began to feel confident that she could face Quinton and be a part of the wedding until Gia called her cell while she was on her way.

"I don't know how you're doing it."

"What are you talking about?"

"You know what I'm talkin' 'bout."

"Oh, Quinton and Melanie? Gia, I have matured. I'm not stuck in the past, and if Quinton and Melanie are happy, then I'm happy for them."

"Okay, but are you happy for yourself?"

"Yes,"

"Girl, you have no man, and you've been celibate for a year. Aren't you a little lonely?"

"Maybe a little bit."

Laila could hear Gia cluck her tongue and she could picture Gia's smirk on her face.

"Okay, okay. I am very lonely. Happy now?" she sighed, "I guess I've been waiting for the right one to come along."

"No, you've been waiting on Quinton to come along, and that bitch, Melanie don' stole that opportunity."

Laila rolled her eyes and pulled into the parking lot of the bridal shop, "Gia, I'm here now. I gotta go. Bye."

"Ah lemme hear-" Laila hung up on her.

Her heart began to beat rapidly as she slowly made her way down the sidewalk. As she opened the door, she took a deep breath and went in. The first person she saw was Quinton gazing at her with a surprised look on his face. This was the first time she laid her eyes on Quinton in eight years. All of her old feelings rushed back and her new revelations completely diminished. He looked even better than his picture in the paper. Handsome dark chocolate skin, a smooth face, and low cut, perfectly lined hair, and a nice build. He stood and they continued to stare for a long time. She slowly walked towards him and broke their gaze.

"Laila, is that you? Wow… aw man… I haven't seen you since high school. Where have you been hiding?"

"Oh, I've been around."

They hugged each other for a long time. She loved the way he felt soft and warm. He smelled good; he was wearing Laila's favorite cologne, Curve. Men in the past had always tried to impress her by wearing overly expensive cologne that they apparently bathed in and then sprayed on their outfits several times. Laila, however, had always been taken by the smell of Curve; it smelled even better on Quinton. It matched his body chemistry perfectly.

"You look different," he said and she wrinkled her

face, "Well, I guess you could say the same about me."

"Yeah," she exhaled, "we're all grown up now."

"You look good girl."

"Thank you. You don't look too bad yourself."

Laila broke their stare and admired the countless lined racks of white and cream wedding gowns each wrapped in plastic. Faceless white mannequins on platforms were scattered throughout the boutique displaying the more expensive dresses intricately stitched to perfection and adorned in lace, pearls, diamonds, and sheer. Laila could picture herself wearing one of the beautiful wedding gowns and marching down the aisle to her very own happily-ever-after.

While sitting on the blue velvet sofa, Quinton talked about how he didn't know Laila had a new house blocks from his mother's house and asked her a few questions. Laila noticed that Melanie kept many details of her life hidden from him, and he didn't seem to mind. Laila was in awe; she kept staring at him in a daze and could barely hear what he was saying. Then, his next statement came from nowhere.

"Do you ever think about us? You know, what could have been?"

She shook her head out of her daze. She began to breathe heavily and was confused. *He's asking about us, when his fiancée is just feet away trying on a wedding dress for their wedding!*

"What?" she looked at him strangely. She couldn't believe what she was hearing. *Melanie!*

Then, she looked around and then back at him. "Is this some kind of test or something?"

He seemed puzzled, "Huh? I-"

"Melanie put you up to this, didn't she? She wanted to see if I was really over you, and you're playing right along with her. Wait until I get my hands on her," she got up, but he held her arm.

"No, no, no. I was just curious. I'm sorry if you

thought I crossed the line."

She could tell that it was something he did not want Melanie knowing he was thinking about. She slowly sat down and sighed. "I thought about it from time to time."

"Really?"

"Yep, but you're about to marry my best friend, so I have no feelings for you now."

Why did he ask me that question?

She looked back at him and he was staring at her. "What?"

"You're… you're just so beautiful," he said looking as if he was in a daze.

Laila didn't know how to respond. "Uh, thank you."

They stared at each other until Melanie interrupted.

"What do you think?" she was strutting down the hall. They quickly looked at her. Her eyes widened when she saw Laila.

"Hi darling, I'm glad you could make it today," she said, then stood on a platform and stared in a three-way mirror.

"Yes, I told you I would."

"Excellent," she said, "So how do I look?"

"Oh, that dress is gorgeous."

"Yeah honey. I love that one," Quinton said.

"Um, I-I- Isn't it bad luck for the groom to see the bride in her dress before the wedding ceremony?" Laila asked.

"Oh, no, it's only if you see the bride the night before the wedding," Melanie said.

"No, I'm pretty sure-"

"Besides, it's all just superstition," she said, "Right, honey?"

"Exactly babe."

Laila felt a sharp pain in her chest and took a deep breath.

Melanie looked at herself in the mirror, running her hands down the dress, "Yes, I feel good about this."

CHAPTER 5

On the night of the engagement party, Laila had finished getting dressed and was fixing her curls in her living room mirror when Gia beeped her horn. Laila rushed out and hopped in Gia's shiny custom-painted candy apple red Mazda6.

"Where's Kecia? I thought we all were going to ride to the party together," she said as she got in and closed the door.

"That was the plan, but she decided to take ol' stank ass with her," she said as she pulled off.

"Oh no, Leonard's coming?" Laila groaned.

"Yep," Gia said.

"Ugh, I don't know what she sees in him."

"Hmm, wasn't your last *four* men just like him?"

"Oh, don't try to *do* me, Ms. Gia. They were successful businessmen who worked in downtown Atlanta, not some broke down car salesman from a small town."

"Daaaamn," Gia laughed.

Laila shook her head. "Uh, I didn't mean that,"

"Oh, yes ya did."

"Uh, you're always rubbing off on me."

Kecia and Gia had always had their way of influencing

Laila's behavior no matter what she tried to do.

"Whatever, you know you ghetto just like me. I don't know why you put on that bourgeois front."

"It's not a front and I'm not bourgeois."

"I'm just saying, you and Melanie used to be right there with me and Kecia chillin' under the carport, eatin' potted meat and saltine crackers."

"Ugh, don't remind me," Laila giggled.

"So, um," she pursed her lips, "how did you feel when you saw Quinton today?"

"Um, okay,"

"Come on, be real. You still like him or not?"

"Well, I was attracted to him."

"Oh, here we go again. Girl, he still don't look any better than he did in high school."

"Whatever, he is sexy. Um, he smelled so good. I just loved the way his chocolate skin-"

"Time out. I heard enough of this Quinton shit in high school, okay?"

"Okay."

"Where was Melanie when you were drooling all over her man?"

"I wasn't drooling and she was in the dressing room."
Gia shook her head.

"He asked me the most peculiar thing though."

"And that was?"

"If I ever thought about him and me."

"Aw, no he didn't,"

"Yeah, I told him, from time to time,"

"And no *you* didn't. You shoulda told that no good animal he never crossed yo' mind. He shouldn't have even known you remembered his name. In all of these years, Laila, have you remembered anything I taught you? When was he thinking 'bout you? The first time he saw Melanie again? The first time he came to her apartment? Or, how bout the first time he stuck dat *D* in her? Did your name ring a bell then? What the he-"

"Okay, I get it," Laila said, "Though he wasn't thinking about me then, we can't overlook the fact that he's thinking about me now."

"That's because he saw your face and saw you looking fine as hell," she held her hand up as if she was solemnly swearing, "no homo, and Melanie probably look like Chewbacca to him now. I know that's what she look like to me."

"Um,"

"So what you gon' do? Get with him?"

"What? No."

"Ooo, yeah. You should break them up before the wedding. That way you can have your man. Ooo... and that way we all won't have to suffer through this wedding."

"No, I'm not stealing anyone. What Quinton and I had was in the past. He's free to move forward with Melanie. I'll find my prince someday."

"Okay, *Princess*. You might as well make that punk ass frog your prince since he's the only one you ever wanted since you were like 14."

"Yea, that is too long to hold a torch for someone."

"Okay, Ima pretend you just didn't say that."

"Say what?"

"I declare. I can't say any of my old country sayings, but Melanie's uppity ass is facing some damn music while Laila's holding a damn torch. What the hell?"

"Hmmm, you've been awfully testy lately. Your friend Rico hasn't been delivering on your *benefits* plan?" Laila smiled. Gia glared at her.

The ladies soon pulled up to a beautiful two-story house. Cars were parked along the curved driveway and in the yard. They could hear music blasting from the backyard. Laila and Gia entered, and the spacious home was filled with guests. They inched their way through the crowd and spoke to people as they passed by.

"Laila, Gia, over here," Melanie called and motioned

for them. She was sitting with Quinton's mother and a man in his late 50's.

"This is my maid of honor, Laila. And this is one of my bridesmaids, Gia."

"Oh nice to meet you girls, I'm Carol and this is my friend, Gary."

"Oh, nice to meet you sir," they all shook hands.

"You girls are beautiful."

"Thank you."

"Wait a minute. Gia?" Carol thought of the name, "You own that hair salon in town?"

"Yes ma'am."

"Aww, a business woman. How impressive. It makes me proud to see young people doing something good with their lives," Gary said.

Carol added. "You keep it up. I still go to Glenda Leakes. She's been styling my hair for fifteen years now."

"Yeah, she's good. She wanted me to work for her when I first got my license to gain more experience, but I had my eye on a bigger prize."

"Aw, and ambitious."

"Uh, will you excuse me," Melanie said. She gave a fake smile. She always hated when people took their focus off her and placed it on her friends, especially Gia.

Carol stared at Laila. "And you, you look so familiar."

"Well, I work at H&L Financial Bank,"

"Oh really."

"That's nice baby."

"What you do there?"

"Oh, I am the director of diversity relations and a loan officer."

"Oh, so they have you wearing many hats."

"You're the only black girl there?"

"No, not anymore."

"Well, it looks like you're doing your job then, but I've never been to that bank before. I can't place where I've seen you before."

"Um, we all were in the same class as Quinton. Maybe you remember me from sch-"

"Well, you know Laila used to date Quinton, but shhh, don't tell anyone."

They looked in shock at Laila.

Laila smiled coyly. "Excuse us," she grabbed Gia's arm and pulled her away.

"What the hell is wrong with you?"

"What?"

"Why did you tell his mother we dated?"

"Well, I'm trying to help you sabotage this wedding."

"Gia, I do not want Quinton anymore. Okay?"

"Okay, but I didn't see anything wrong with me telling. If you weren't into him anymore, you wouldn't have cared either, but since you *are*, you're having a big fit."

"I'm not having a fit. I just don't want her looking at me all under-eyed like she used to whenever she saw me and Quinton with Marla somewhere nearby."

"Well, my bad, you never know she might be *your* mother-in-law someday."

"I think that perm has fried your brain because you're crazy right now."

"Really, I thought it was the weed I just smoked," Gia started laughing, "Naw, I'm just playing you know I don't smoke."

"This is not a joking matter, Gia,"

"Hey y'all," Kecia came up.

"Thank goodness," Laila looked at her, "Will you tame Gia?"

"Girl, you know I can't be tamed."

"What she do now?"

"The question is what hasn't she done? She went over there and told Quinton's mother about him and I."

"Gia, no."

"I mean it's no big secret."

Laila looked towards the front door. "Where is Leonard?"

"He had a business call, so I left his ass. I told him he can come later on if he wanted to."

"Ooo, he's not gonna be mad that you left him, is he?" Laila asked. She was afraid that they may start fussing as they often did.

"Girl, naw."

"Oh, there you girls are," Melanie said, "Follow me." She looked excited. She led them to the backyard and that's when they saw Quinton, David, Taaz, among the crowd of guests.

"Here are the girls."

"Hey ladies,"

"Oh hey Quinton," Gia said, "Hey, Taaz wit yo' little punk ass."

"Aite, I got your punk right here," he said. He and Kecia gazed at each other, and both rolled their eyes. The girls didn't acknowledge the other guys that were standing with them.

"You girls haven't changed a bit," Quinton said.

"So these are the groomsmen. We're only missing Alonzo. I just saw Chuck a minute ago, and girls, I'll be having two more bridesmaids which are Quinton's younger cousins," then she whispered to them, "They're 21."

"Why didn't you girls come to the class reunion?" Quinton asked.

They had a reunion already? I didn't know.

"I have my own business. I didn't have time for all of that," Gia said.

"I heard that," David finally said. He was always the quiet one in the group and the girls never paid him any mind.

"Yeah, I remember Kecia and Laila taking every chance they got to get away from our class."

"Yep, and that's why I didn't go to no lame ass reunion," Kecia said.

"It's called a ten-year class reunion anyway. Not six or

eight but ten. We don't wanna see nobody else's ass in our class until the full ten years is up."

"I know right," Kecia said.

Quinton shook his head. "Gia, I have been hearing a lot of good things about your shop," he said placing his hands in his pockets.

"Oh yes honey. I've got the best shop in town. The latest equipment, I make sure my place is kept up very well, and I treat my customers like family unless, of course, a bitch gets on my nerves."

"Well, if you need any help with advertising or even if you would like some marketing material such as brochures to give your clientele, I'm your man,"

"Okay," she smiled. Then looked at Melanie, "You hear that Melanie? Quinton's *my* man." She laughed.

"Honey, you wish," Melanie said holding his arm.

Kecia looked at Laila, and said dryly, "Hmm, don't we all. I'm about to get me a plate. I'll be back."

Taaz followed her to the table as she looked at the countless rows of food.

"I see you still be gettin' your grub on,"

"Taaz, I thought I had dodged your little ass,"

"Oh, so that's whatcha been doin' all this time?"

"Basically,"

"Aw come on now," Taaz said, "You can't possibly still be thinking about our fights in high school."

"No, unlike some people, I don't dwell in the past," she said, "And from that outfit, it looks like you're still living in the 90s."

"Oh, so you wanna talk about my clothes. You know what? I thought I had saw you earlier."

She turned and looked at him.

"You were laying on the table looking all scrumptious, then I realized it was just a roasted pig."

"And still lame, I see." She rolled her eyes and walked off.

Gia came up to Taaz, "Taaz, you ain't over here tryna

mess wit Kecia again, are ya?"

"Naw, I ain't said nothin' to her."

"Oh, I was bout to say…I was finna get ready to cut you."

"You need to finally let me hit that."

"Now, Taaz you know you've always loved you some big luscious thick women."

"No, the hell I don't."

"Hmm, that cheerleader from Eastwood High,"

"Who?"

"And Quinton's cousin, Porsha,"

"Man, that girl was skinny back then. She just had a huge ass."

"And Kecia."

"What? I ain't never liked her. Ugh,"

"Whatever, Taaz."

Meanwhile, Laila was still standing with Melanie, Quinton, and his friends.

"So um, Laila, you seeing anybody?" David asked.

"No, I've just been enjoying being single."

"Ain't nothing wrong with that," another guy named Al said.

"I'm going to fix her up as soon as we get back from our honeymoon."

Laila tilted her head and quickly looked at her. "Melanie, excuse me, but I don't need to be fixed up by anyone. I said I was enjoying being single, so that means I have no plans to date any time soon, okay?"

Melanie looked at her strangely, "O-kay."

"Um, catfight," Jamal, one of Quinton's groomsmen, said under his breath.

"All I want is for you to find happiness like I have," Melanie said.

"Well, I have myself covered just fine, okay?"

"I said okay," Melanie said softly not looking at her.

Quinton intervened, "Yeah, leave the girl alone. I'm sure some man will come along and sweep her off her feet."

She had let him slide earlier but this was neither the time nor the place. She had to say something. Her head quickly whipped in Quinton's direction and she frowned, "Girl? Did you just call me girl?"

"I-"

"This *woman* respectfully has a name and it's *Laila*."

"Ooo," the fellas said.

"Well, I'm sorry."

Embarrassed, Melanie gently held Laila's arm and looked at the guys. "Can you excuse us?" Then, pulled her away.

The guys looked at each other and said simultaneously, "PMS."

"What was that, Laila?"

"I don't care if Quinton is your man, fiancé, or whatever, but we all went to high school together and I'm not about to have him disrespecting me. He didn't disrespect me back then, and he is not going to start now."

"Well, Laila. I'm sure he didn't mean any harm by it. It was simply a slip of the tongue. He was trying to defend you."

Laila rolled her eyes and crossed her arms.

"Are you okay?"

"Yes, I'm fine," she walked off and passed by Kecia and Gia, completely ignoring them.

"Laila," they called, but she continued towards the house.

"Well, somebody don' pissed her off."

"What's Laila's problem?" Melanie asked.

"What happened?"

"She started going off on me and Quinton."

Their eyes grew wide. "Ooo, about what?" they said in unison.

"Well long story short. Quinton called her girl," she said.

"Oooo,"

"No, his ass didn't," Gia said.

"I mean all he said was leave the girl alone when I was trying to fix her up on a blind date."

"What?" Kecia said, "You don't make her look desperate to have a man in front of all those men."

"Well, I know she's not desperate."

"And Quinton hasn't seen us in years and thinks he can talk to us like we've been around him every day?"

"Oh, he gon' have to do some apologizing. Laila don't play no man calling her anything outside of her name. They gotta be real cool before she let that go down," Gia said.

"Really? I didn't know she was like that now."

"Yeah girl. Just have Quinton talk to her, she'll be alright," Gia said. Kecia cut her eyes at Gia, knowing she was trying to get the two alone.

"Okay, that's a great idea because there cannot be any tension between my groom and maid of honor."

Taaz was still standing outside in the backyard with David while Kecia was admiring the tables of food once again. She finally picked up a plate. She dressed her plate with barbecue ribs, a T-bone steak, a chicken leg, a hot dog, a burger, baked beans mixed with beef and bell peppers, and potato salad.

"I know you like a book," Leonard came up to her with a smug look on his face. "Where there's a food table, there's Kecia Jones."

Taaz and David were staring at them. Taaz smirked, "So that's her punk ass boyfriend. Humph…"

"As soon as I walked through the door, I asked the hostess where the food was located and it led me straight to you," Leonard chuckled.

She paid him no mind. "Yeah whatever… you want me to fix you-"

"Look at your plate."

He took her plate, beans spilling to the ground, and threw the entire plate in the trash next to him.

Taaz gasped and placed his fist to his mouth, "Man, don't he know that was a death sentence? You don't grab no food from Kecia... Oh, we bout to see the Hulk up in this mother-"

Taaz and David came closer for a front row view of the match between Kecia and Leonard.

"Leonard, I will not tolerate you disrespecting me in public," she said speaking in a low tone filled with menace, so she would not bring attention to herself but still let Leonard know she was serious.

"Aw, calm down. I'm going to fix you another plate, baby. Just have a seat or find your friends, I will bring your new plate to you. I love you."

She stormed away, looked up, and noticed Taaz and David looking at her. David quickly looked in another direction, but Taaz was looking at her in disbelief.

"What the hell kind of –"

"Don't even say it," she said to Taaz as she walked by.

In the house, Laila, holding her fourth glass of wine in her hand, slid past guests in the hallway. She saw Quinton inching through the crowd and noticed a few people congratulating him. She tried to go in the opposite direction before he could reach her, but he placed his hand on her shoulder. With a smirk on her face, she turned to look at him.

"Can I talk to you for a minute?" he asked. She shrugged and he led her into the upstairs bathroom and locked the door.

"Laila, what was that really about outside?"

"Nothing. Why?"

"I know you just didn't get upset over the word, *girl*,"

"Well, yes. I felt like you were treating me like I'm some stranger now," she sighed and stared him in the eye, "Look, I'm tolerating the fact that you're with Melanie and I'm tolerating this role of maid of honor at this we, we— wedding, but I can't tolerate you treating me like we never were anything to each other even if we were just kids back then."

"You're tolerating? So, you don't like the fact that Melanie and I are together?"

"Of course not."

He bit his bottom lip, "you still have feelings for me?"

She sighed, "I don't know. I just know I always wanted to be with you, but now, I won't get a chance because you decided to go around the world and then marry one of my closest friends."

"I'm sorry. I wasn't expecting to fall for her honestly."

"Well, one thing is obvious. When you two crossed paths again, you had forgotten about me. I know that now, so it's fine."

"Laila, I'm sorry. If I thought there was a chance that you and I could have been together, I would have never given Melanie a second thought. I just thought you had your own thing going, so I didn't want to mess it up. You know," he shrugged, "Melanie and me just happened. I wasn't trying to hurt you. In fact, I thought you wouldn't care, honestly,"

She blew her breath. "Well, why did you ask me that question in the bridal shop today?"

"If you ever thought about us?"

Laila nodded.

"I don't know, maybe because all of these memories and feelings flooded my mind as soon as you walked in," Laila's heart skipped a beat. He felt the same way she did. "Laila, you're a beautiful woman, I can't deny that. What I said… It was… it was just an error in judgment, and I apologize for that."

"Okay."

"I just want to make sure that you're comfortable with being a part of the wedding because I'll understand if you don't want to participate."

Laila exhaled. "No, I'm okay now."

"I know it's hard to say no to Melanie sometimes, but I don't want any animosity between us that would keep this occasion from being a joyful one for Melanie."

What about you?

"No, we're fine, Quinton."

"Okay, I believe you," he said, "So, friends?" He held out his hand.

"Friends," she shook his hand.

"Aw come here," he hugged her. They held each other. Laila closed her eyes and inhaled deeply, taking in his scent. She could feel him taking in her delicate fragrance as well. They slowly pulled back, looking into each other's eyes. They received a knock on the door and jumped.

"Hey, who's in my private bathroom?" They heard an older woman's raspy voice say. They quickly broke away from their embrace.

"Aunt Sarah, it's me, Quinton."

"Oh, okay, baby. Just making sure it's my blood and no one else," she said through the door. "We're wine tasting for your wedding. Come on baby. We've been in the cellar waiting for you, especially your mother and fiancée." He remembered his aunt and uncle had invited them to sample their wine collection before the party began. He waited until he heard her bedroom door close before he spoke. He touched the small of Laila's back.

"Are you okay?"

She nodded. "Just gonna wait here for a few minutes."

"Good idea," he said, then rushed out. Laila sat on the side of the tub and sighed.

CHAPTER 6

Laila barely remembered what she and Quinton said in the bathroom or how she ended up in the backseat of Gia's car, but she knew she had to try to let him go and support Melanie. It was the next day and she had just gotten off work. She dreaded going to the place that the happy couple would share their vows.

When she arrived to the church for rehearsal, Melanie's aunt, Judy, made everyone take their places around the altar, but the best man, Alonzo, was nowhere to be found. Quinton and Alonzo had been best friends since they were babies. In high school, they were inseparable and all the girls had to have them. The two would usually date sisters and best friends. Their most exclusive relationships were with Marla Gomillion and Alexandra Reid, the captains of the cheerleading squad.

Alonzo was someone that Laila loathed since she first transferred to the school in the 7th grade. He was pompous, arrogant, and thought he was God's gift to every woman. He was like a big kid, but his demeanor had always spelled debonair. She remembered him being a player in high school, and girls melting at the sight of him. She thought it was sick because the girls knew exactly how he was yet they still wanted to be with him only because he was *so fine.* She despised the way females treated him like a celebrity, like he was the sexiest man alive. Maybe Matt Damon and George Clooney didn't get that memo. Even Laila couldn't deny the fact that he was very nice looking, but she couldn't understand what was so amazing about him. A light- skinned guy with chestnut brown eyes and wavy black hair? What's the big deal? Well, many girls in high school wondered the same about her, *what do they see in that yellow curly haired goody two shoes?*

"Okay, let's get to it," Aunt Judy interrupted her thoughts.

Laila frowned. She had never been a big fan of Melanie's aunt. She always wanted to have control over everything, and she would get mad if she didn't get her way. When her ex-husband died, she wanted to be the mistress of ceremony, and was angered when his wife said no. Then, she grew even more upset when her name wasn't mentioned in the obituary. Even though Laila's parents were no longer in her life, she still wanted nothing to do with Melanie's aunt because she didn't want her to try to control any aspect of her life.

After Aunt Judy's divorce, she never remarried and she gave Melanie a home when no one else would. She did the best she could while working two jobs. She never let Melanie go anywhere except to Laila or Kecia's house. Melanie was not allowed to spend the night with Gia under any circumstance because she had four brothers living with her.

At that time, Melanie was very promiscuous and Aunt Judy sheltering her made her even worse. She would sneak boys into the house when her aunt was at work or she would lie about spending the night with Laila, so she could be with some guy all night. Her control drove Melanie to take drastic measures to get what she wanted and she always did. Laila had to admit there was one thing about Aunt Judy's control issues: she got things done. She looked around the church. The only hindrance at that point was Alonzo.

Alonzo had always been about himself. He did things when he wanted to do them, and he didn't care who had anything to say about it. Laila thought maybe he had grown up, but it seemed as if he was up to his same old ways. She hadn't seen him much since high school. He was living in Atlanta for a while, and he just moved back in town not too long ago. She often saw his silver Mercedes, with tint so dark it had to be illegal, passing by the bank. He had opened up an account the week before, when Laila was out to lunch. When she came back, he was gone and all of the women were talking about how handsome he was.

"They need to hurry up," Gia and Kecia were standing beside her. They were more agitated than anybody. Kecia was missing out on time with Leonard, and Gia was missing out on earning cash from her after-hour appointments that she rescheduled.

"Dang man, where is Alonzo?" They heard Taaz ask Quinton.

"I don't know."

"It's just like Alonzo to make people wait like the world revolves around him," Kecia said.

"Um huh, same old Alonzo," Gia said.

"I'm sorry everyone. We're just waiting on my best man," Quinton announced.

"Where is he?" Melanie asked.

"He said he had to run to the ATL on business, but he should have been back by now."

At that moment, the church doors opened and Alonzo made his way down the aisle.

"Damn!" Kecia, Gia, and another bridesmaid said. Alonzo had grown from a cute boy into a handsome man. His light skin was now a sexy red like he'd been kissed by the sun.

With an impeccable build and an arrogant swagger,

Alonzo Davis looked majestic and he was obviously delighted that everyone around him acknowledged it. He was well-groomed with fresh baby twists and a well-trimmed, closely-shaved beard. He had a confident stride in his walk as he flaunted his charcoal gray pin-striped suit. The room commanded his attention and he enjoyed every minute. Laila looked at him, rolled her eyes, and looked toward Quinton as everyone was still watching Alonzo slowly make his way to his spot.

"Sorry, I'm late man," he said, "You know how it is."

"Yeah, man,"

"Hmm, looking good," Melanie said. He smiled at her.

"Thanks cuz,"

"Uh, don't flatter him baby. His head is already big enough," she shook her head and then turned away to speak to her aunt.

Taaz hit Alonzo's arm, "Man, what took you so long?"

"You know me, always fashionably late," he straightened his suit, "But for real though, my meeting ran a bit longer than expected."

"Umm huh, we know all about your *meetings*," Taaz said. He smacked hands with David and chuckled while Alonzo and Quinton simply shook their heads.

"Okay, let's get started," Aunt Judy announced. Meanwhile, Gia and Kecia were still staring at Alonzo.

"Dang, I wouldn't mind getting with that," Gia said.

"Girl, a ho is gon' always be a ho. Look at him now. You know he ain't about to change for nobody."

"Uh huh."

Alonzo adjusted his tie and glanced around the room until Laila caught his eye. He stared at Laila as the bridal party made their way down the aisle. He noticed the girls staring at him and a big grin came across his face. He pointed at the two, waved and raised his brows at Kecia to let her know he was impressed with what he saw. They pursed their lips and waved back at him.

"Did you just see the way he was looking at Laila?"

Kecia leaned over to Gia.

"Yeah, I saw."

"Quinton and Alonzo are both feeling Laila. Then, Quinton is supposed to be marrying Melanie. This should be an interesting wedding."

"Girl, you ain't never lied," Gia said. Soon, the girls were waiting in the lobby while Melanie was sitting in an adjacent room.

"Okay, men. When the ladies walk down the aisle, they're going to already have a bouquet in their hands."

"Duh, is this bitch dumb?"

"Shh..." Kecia said as the other bridesmaids giggled.

Laila felt like she was in a daze, standing at the front doors of the church while the man she always wanted stood at the altar. She noticed Alonzo gawking at her, licking his lips, and rubbing the corners of his mouth with his thumb and index finger. She rolled her eyes and hid herself behind Gia.

Still speaking to the groomsmen, Aunt Judy instructed, "I want you to meet her with your right hand behind your back at this front pew. In your right hand will be a single cut white rose. Take her hand, bow, come closer, look passionately into her eyes, and draw the rose from behind your back and place it in her hair on the left side. Then, interlock arms and escort her to the appropriate spot."

Taaz had his complaints too. "Damn, why is she making us do all of this and why did they pair me up with big Kecia? I don't want to be looking all in her damn eyes. She shoulda put Kecia with big Chuck over there."

They looked over at Chuck and he was in his own world, looking up at the ceiling. He sniffed and smelled under his arms. Jamal, who was on his cell phone, shook his head at Chuck.

"Yes, a real class act," Alonzo said sarcastically.

"Come on, she's Melanie's aunt. Just do it man for your boy."

"Okay, now that we have it," Aunt Judy said, "Let's

begin."

The bridesmaids and the groomsmen began rehearsing. When Kecia and Taaz met, he grinned at her and she frowned at him.

Laila slowly walked down the aisle. She felt nervous and her heart began to beat rapidly. She was supposed to walk alone to her spot, but Alonzo met her.

"Alonzo, what are you doing man? The maid of honor is supposed to walk alone."

"I know, Quinton, but a woman this beautiful deserves to be escorted."

Aunt Judy raised her brows as Laila shook her head and smiled. He took Laila's hand and planted a gentle kiss. She was surprised at how nice his warm, soft lips felt against her hand. Then, he looked passionately into her eyes. She couldn't believe he was trying to be suave with her once again. She decided to play right along with him, so she gave him a sexy stare right back.

"Yes!" Melanie's aunt interrupted the rehearsal. "That's the kind of intensity that I want to see. Y'all need to watch them."

"We need you to kiss our ass." Gia said and Kecia hit her.

"You're right! We should add that kiss too."

"Hell naw," Taaz blurted.

"You two do that again."

Laila was tired of being timid, shy, and anxious so she decided to be bold. She slightly switched her hips as she walked down the aisle and all of the men's eyes were on her.

"Showin' out," Gia smiled and Kecia watched in surprise.

"Work it girl," one of the other bridesmaids said. Taaz made all kinds of noises and Alonzo stood at the front pew watching her until she disappeared behind the door. Then, Alonzo quickly went and stood by Quinton, who had a solemn look on his face. The two met once again, he kissed her hand, and they stared into each other's eyes. She had never looked into his eyes for longer than a few seconds. She noticed his eyes had a sparkle to them.

"Yes, yes. Intensity. Passion. Desire. Love. Those are emotions I want to see," Aunt Judy said with excitement.

Quinton began to roll his eyes and blow his breath. Gia nudged Kecia to look at him.

"Uhh huh," they both said.

Once Laila and Alonzo were finally in place, Melanie came down the aisle, smiling from ear-to-ear with her eyes completely on Quinton.

"Now, that's love right there," One bridesmaid said to the other.

"Uh," Gia said, "Who are those bitches behind you again?"

"I don't know."

"Okay, now I'm going to do a quick run through," The pastor cleared his throat.

"Dearly beloved we are gathered here today to witness these two unite in holy matrimony etcetera, etcetera. Then I'm going to motion for you two to turn and face each other. Then, you are going to recite your vows," Quinton and Melanie faced each other.

"Well, I don't have anything prepared right now, so I'll say something from the heart. Quinton, I truly love you with all of my heart. You're my entire life. My life is complete and my happiest moments are with you. I don't know what I would do if you weren't by my side. You are the rain, I am but a seed. Both God and you are my sunlight, you both feed me, I've bloomed, and have grown into a beautiful, delicate flower."

"Ain't that Beyoncé?!" Gia exclaimed. Kecia nudged her to be quiet.

"No, it's not,"

Laila almost laughed, remembering "Dangerously in Love" was Melanie's favorite song, and then Quinton looked at her and quickly at Melanie. All of a sudden, her throat felt dry and scratchy. She coughed and cleared her throat. Quinton swallowed.

"Quinton, I really and truly love you," he looked at Laila again who was standing right behind Melanie. It was hard for him not to look at her. She started coughing again and everyone looked at her.

"Oh, excuse me."

Then, Melanie turned back to Quinton, and he began to recite his impromptu vows, "You make my whole life complete. When I think of the perfect woman, I think of you because you are the only one for me."

At that moment, her coughs became uncontrollable. She began to turn red and Gia started patting her on her back. Speaking through her coughs, "I'm just gonna get a sip of water," she hurried down the aisle.

"Must be the weather," Melanie smiled.

"Oh, it's the weather alright," Kecia said under her breath.

Laila was standing at the water cooler, taking a huge gulp from her cone shaped cup.

"So after all of this time, you still have feelings for Q."

She turned around and saw Alonzo smiling back at her. "No, I don't." She tossed the cup in the trash.

"Then, why all of sudden you have this cough attack when he professes his love for your friend in front of God and everyone?"

She shrugged. "I'm just not feeling well today, Alonzo. That is all."

"Okay. Do you need me to drive you home?"

"No," she snapped.

They heard Aunt Judy say, "Well everyone. That's enough for today. I have to run to Wal-Mart. We'll do another rehearsal on Wednesday. I have some changes that need to be made."

"Now if you'll excuse me," she walked passed him and tripped over the mat on the floor. Alonzo held in his laugh, smiled and shook his head. Never looking back at him, she opened up the doors of the church and rushed out.

CHAPTER 7

"Well, well, well. Marla Gomillion," Melanie and Quinton, with a cart full of groceries, party favors, and decorations, ended up in Marla Gomillion's checkout line at Wal-Mart. "I didn't know you were a cashier. You had so much potential. What happened?"

Quinton raised his brows. His cell vibrated just in time, and he quickly answered as he placed the items on the conveyor belt. Marla looked at her with a blank expression. She was not in the mood for Melanie's arrogant bitchiness. She sighed and decided to interact without losing her composure, so she could keep her job.

"It's called life."

"Hmm, really?"

"Yep, in this world, you have to do what you have to do in order to make a living."

"Wow, you almost sound like a stripper."

Marla paused and glared at her. *Oh now this bitch is pushing it.* She frowned. "What the hell did you just say?"

"So um, Taaz…" Quinton turned away, trying to stay out of the girls' spat.

"Oh, nothing. I just thought, you know, since the boys were looking for a stripper for the bachelor party, I thought maybe you knew som-"

"Whatever, Melanie," Marla rolled her eyes.

"So are you married? Any kids?" she smirked, "Baby daddies?"

"No, I'm single and I don't have any children," she said in pure aggravation.

She looked at Quinton and he wasn't paying her any attention. He was still glued to his phone, doing his best not to participate in the girls' conversation.

"Hey Quinton. Long time no see."

He looked at her. "Oh, hey Marla," he quickly said and continued his phone conversation as he put the bags into the cart. Melanie smiled in delight.

"I saw you two were getting married in the paper. Congratulations."

"Thank you. You can come if you'd like."

"Oh, how thoughtful, but no thanks," she said sarcastically, "That will be $182.50."

"Honey, I'll be in the car," Quinton said. He kissed her on the cheek as she got her credit card out of her purse. Marla watched as Quinton walked off pushing the cart full of bags.

"From the way your friend, *Lena* was chasing Quinton when I was with him, I would have thought for sure he would be marrying her."

It irked Melanie how Marla had always purposely mispronounced their names ever since high school. Melanie swiped her credit card, keyed in her pin, and Marla pressed the credit key.

"Well, he's marrying me and *Laila* is happy for me."

"Whatever you say," she handed Melanie the receipt, and Melanie snatched it from her.

"You have a nice life as a *cashier*," she walked off.

Soon, Melanie and Quinton were riding around town in his black Yukon Denali. They both were on their phones. Quinton looked over at her and smiled; she blew a kiss at him. Melanie ended her call, pulled down the visor, and looked at herself in the mirror. When they reached a stop sign, Quinton spotted Laila. She was in the parking lot, walking towards the bank. Her long curly hair was let down. She had on cream pants, heels, and a black dressy sleeveless top showing her cleavage. She was carrying a cream blazer in her arms and he stared at her every move. His mouth was wide open, and his phone slipped out of his hands.

A car horn beeped behind him. Then, Melanie started looking around.

"Ooo, there's Laila. Pull in," he made a right at the stop sign and a left into the parking lot.

He obeyed. She quickly got out, and Quinton quickly found his phone.

"Ah Taaz, you still there?" he stared at Laila, "Oh my bad. I dropped my phone."

Melanie came up to Laila. "Hey girl," she said as she hugged her friend. Laila did not look happy to see her. "Look at you."

"I wasn't expecting to see you just now."

Melanie got the hint that her friend did not want to be bothered, but she thought Laila was hiding something, so she grew suspicious, "What are you up to?"

"Oh, I'm just getting back from lunch."

"Really? So they let you wear tops like that to work?"

"Girl, no. I just pulled off my jacket because I was hot."

"You surely are," she touched her arm, "Ouch!" Melanie shook her hand and they both smiled yet Laila's was a forced smile.

Melanie asked her. "So what are you doing tonight?"

Quinton's eyes were still on Laila, he stared at her beautiful face. He admired the way the breeze slightly blew her hair. His eyes inched from her head down to her toes. He couldn't stop himself from admiring her breasts. His mouth began to water as he licked his lips. His hand was trembling, trying to hold his phone steady to his ear.

Taaz said, "Tasia is trippin' for real. I gotta pick up the kids from school today."

"Oh for real?"

Quinton could hear Taaz's rambling speech, but he paid his friend's words no mind.

"Ummm, uh, umm," Quinton moaned as he continued gazing at her. He could feel his member harden, "Damn."

"Ugh, man!" Taaz said in disgust, "Is Melanie sucking your dick right now?"

"What?" Quinton sat up, "Naw, man. I was just … I was just looking at something."

"Yeah right, man," Taaz said. "Ah, I'll holla atcha later."

"Alright," he placed his phone in the cup holder.

He watched Laila as she put on her blazer; she gazed at him as she was talking to Melanie. Then he looked down and saw just how hard he was.

"Damn," he said as he held himself. He tried to calm himself down before Melanie came back.

Laila was busy trying to make up an excuse, so she wouldn't have to spend time with Melanie. "Oh, I have so much to do tonight," she said as she dug in her purse and pulled out a hair clamp to pin her hair back up.

"Oh, okay. Well, I promised Aunt Judy that I was going to spend the night with her tonight. You can stop by if you have some time."

"Oh okay. I'll think about it," she felt Quinton's eyes on her once again, and decided to wave at him. He slowly waved back. She quickly made her way into the bank as Melanie made her way back to Quinton.

She got in the truck.

"Honey, are you okay?"

"Yeah, I'm fine."

"Oh, you look flustered. Did Taaz -"

"Oh no, don't worry about it, *bae*. I got it."

"Oh okay."

He licked his lips as he pulled back onto the street. "So

um, you're still going to meet me at Hudson Creek tomorrow, right?"

"Oh yeah," she began checking herself out in the mirror once again.

"Because the last time I asked you, you were completely against it."

"Oh no, I'm fine. I'll do anything for you, darling," she leaned over and kissed him on the cheek and then looked back into the vanity mirror while putting on pink lipstick. "I wouldn't miss it for the world."

CHAPTER 8

Kecia was sitting in her classroom. All 33 of her children were writing in their journals when the intercom buzzed.

"Ms. Jones," a young black woman's voice flooded the room.

"Yes,"

"Someone's here to check out Tyson and Tiana Smith,"

"Okay,"

A light-brown skinned girl with braids pulled in a ponytail with a white ribbon wrapped in a bow got up along with her twin brother who was in the seat on the next row. Then, everyone started moving around.

"Settle down, class. It ain't time to go yet."

"Ooo, Ms. Jones, you said ain't," another girl said.

"Yes, you said there was a time and place for everything, and we're supposed to speak proper English in this class."

"Well, thank you for listening, class," she said, "I apologize for my behavior."

"We accept," they all said.

She shook her head.

"Oh, I almost forgot. Class, you have a homework

assignment for tonight."

"Aww," they groaned, then Tiana and Tyson sat back down and grabbed their pens and notebooks.

"For your English assignment, read pages 107 to 110 and complete Exercise D on page 112. For your spelling assignment, write a sentence for each of your new spelling words this week. If for some odd reason, you've forgotten your spelling words, refer to page 89 in your Spelling book."

Taaz appeared at the door and knocked. Kecia looked up and was surprised to see him. Tiana and Tyson jumped up and put their pen and notebooks in their book sacks. The rest of the class began to put their things away as well.

"Kecia Jones, they let *you* be an English teacher?"

"Tazmon, I am an excellent teacher and the children just love me, don't you class?"

"Yes, Ms. Jones," they said simultaneously.

"Hmm…" Taaz said. Tiana and Tyson came up to him. Tiana hugged him. Kecia observed how the twins look so much like him.

"Y'all wait in the car, Uncle David's out there."

"Okay," Tiana said.

"Bye, Ms. Jones," Tyson said.

"Bye honey,"

The twins walked out.

Kecia looked at her watch, and then looked up at Taaz, "You're cutting it kind of close, aren't you?"

"Yeah, I would have come earlier, but I had to take care of some business,"

"Umm…huh," she gave him an under eyed look. *Chasing women.*

The bell rang and the kids jumped up.

"Don't forget to complete your homework, and don't forget we're having the weekly class spelling bee tomorrow," she called. Taaz watched as the kids walked out of Kecia's classroom in a single file line.

"You got these kids in check, don't ya?"

"They know how to behave with me."

She began to put away her lesson plan and other items on her desk. She looked up to find Taaz still standing in the same spot.

She cleared her throat. "So, you're Tyson and Tiana's father?"

"What? Naw, I'm their uncle," he walked closer to her desk, "Now, you know big swole Leon Hutchins is they daddy."

"Yeah, that's right," she finally remembered.

"Glad they got their looks from me."

"Wait a minute! Tasia Smith is your sister?"

"Yep, half-sister. People had always said we looked alike. I just thought we probably were cousins since we had the same last name. We didn't find out we had the same daddy until a couple of years after graduation."

"Oh, I see," Kecia pulled out her purse from her bottom desk and they made their way to the door and stood.

"So you gon' be at the rehearsal tonight?" he asked.

"They're having another one?"

"You know what? I don't even know. I just guessed."

"Um, I don't know why they keep having rehearsals. One time is enough."

"Sho'll is, but our dumb asses keep showing up."

"Like we have nothing else better to do," she added as she looked around the classroom to make sure everything was in its proper place.

"You know what? I think we're having Quinton's bachelor party," he thought, "...it's either tonight or tomorrow night."

"Hmm...how could that possibly slip your mind?"

Leonard appeared in the doorway and she looked up at him. "Oh, hi honey. What are you doing here?"

"I thought it would be a nice gesture to come pick you up from work."

"Aw, but uh, I came to work in my car."

"Yeah, I thought about that. You can just leave it here for tonight. It'll be safe, then I'll just drop you off in the morning on my way to work."

Taaz raised his brows. Leonard never acknowledged his presence.

"Umm, I have to ask Mr. Brown,"

"What?" Taaz asked. Kecia cut her eyes at him, then Taaz decided to speak, "What's up, man? I'm Taaz."

Leonard just looked at him, then back at Kecia, "Are you ready?"

"You know what?" Taaz said, "She ain't. We were in the middle of a damn um … parent-teacher conference, so give us some *got* damn privacy." Taaz closed the door in his face and locked it. *Got.* It was many Southerners way of *not* using the Lord's name in vain.

Kecia gasped, "Why did you do that, Taaz?"

"What? I don't care… He ain't gon' do shit. What he gon' do to me?"

"Uh, you get on my nerves,"

"And you do too," he said, "Why you let this guy treat you like that? I know I said some messed up stuff to you as a kid but this right here is way beyond that."

"Tazmon," she warned, "stay out of my business."

"Kecia, don't let this cat control you," he studied her face as she avoided eye contact, "I know you ain't scared of him. Hell, you can fling his little ass with your finger."

She quickly looked at him, "Hmm, is that another fat joke?"

"No, it's not. Kecia, wake up, man. Don't leave your car here, so he can control what you do tonight. You do this now; he gon' make sure you end up with no car, so you can depend on him to ride everywhere."

"It's not like that. He knows I'm tired, so he's just-"

"Full of bullshit," he said. There was silence. Taaz paced around the room and glanced out the window. "I know ol' Jerome Hollis be up here at night tryna jack some shit. Man, don't do that."

Kecia blew her breath, "Are we done?"

He bobbed his head and opened the door, "Ladies first," he said to her. She walked out and stood beside an angry Leonard. Taaz eyed him and smirked as he walked down the hall.

"He doesn't know who he's messing with. Who was that anyway?"

Kecia sighed, "A concerned guardian."

"He looks familiar."

"He should. He was at the engagement party the other night. He's in the wedding and my partner to be exact."

"Your partner?"

"Yep, he escorts me down the aisle. Are you jealous?"

"Of him?" he laughed, "Not at all."

They made their way outside.

"Well, I hope you know I ain't leaving my car here overnight. I worked too hard for it to just leave it sitting up anywhere."

"What? So, I came up here for nothing."

"Yes, looks that way," she said, "Besides, I have some *things* I need to do tonight."

"And that is?"

"None of your business."

He tensed.

"See you when I get home," she got in her car and drove off.

CHAPTER 9

"Hi Laila, what are you doing?"

Laila was sitting in her office trying to sort through piles of documents when Melanie called the bank.

"I'm working."

"Oh, really?"

"You know that I work Monday through Friday, and this is my office phone that you just called."

"Oh really, I just-"

"So what do you want, Melanie?"

"I see one thinks she knows one like a book."

"Well, *one* better tell me what she wants before I hang up."

"Well, excuse me, Laila. I see Gia has been highly influencing you at your peak of maturity."

Laila frowned, "I will say this one more time-"

"Okay, okay. Do you think you can take off for a second?"

"Take off? For what?"

"Well, Quinton wanted me to meet him at some secluded country area, and I won't be able to make it."

"And why is that?"

She took a deep breath. "He has his mind set on

taking wedding photos deep in the woods. The woods, Laila," she whispered.

"Well, you know it is his wedding too, Melanie."

"Well, he's not about to drag me in the depths of the dark, cold woods, so I can get bitten by a poisonous snake or break out in hives from the sting of an infectious insect."

Laila noticed Melanie was speaking in her bougie tone with colorful nonsense. "Melanie, who are you with right now?"

"Oh, some girlfriends from college and I are having a get-together. They've hand-stitched favors and other accessories such as the ring bearer's pillow for the wedding which is, of course, a necessity. Rachel, Anna, and Katelyn won't be able to make it to the wedding as they have other engagements, so today is the only time I can visit with them and acquire the beautifully crafted items they made for me."

Laila shook her head.

"So can you?"

"Can I what? You haven't asked me a question. I've been waiting for your question for twenty minutes now."

"Can you please find Quinton in the woods and tell him I won't be able to make it?" Melanie asked, but didn't wait for an answer. She started giving Laila instructions. "Be sincere; tell him my friend is going out of town and I needed to pick up some of our decorations today. I've tried to call and text him, but his phone is not picking up. Please Laila,"

"Melanie, I have to work; you know that I have bills to pay. I can't take off on a whim just to find Quinton."

"Please Laila."

Laila heard her phone vibrate in her purse. *I must have gotten a text.*

"You can run out there for a few seconds and come right back to your job. I just don't want him standing in those dangerous woods all alone waiting for me."

"While you're miles away having tea."

"Exactly."

Laila exhaled, "Okay."

"Thanks Laila. I already sent the directions to your cell. I owe you; love you. Kisses."

She hung up before Laila could respond. Laila shook her head, grabbed her purse, and headed out of her office door.

She drove along a path and saw Quinton's black SUV and pulled beside it. She got out of the car; he appeared from behind the trees.

"Hi, Laila. I wasn't expecting to see you," he said nervously.

"Yeah,"

He sighed. "Let me guess. She cancelled on me."

"Yeah, that pretty much sums it up."

"I should have known. I haven't been able to get any service out here," he said looking at his phone, "While you're here, can you check out the spot so you can tell your friend how much she's overreacting?"

"Um, I have to get back to work."

"Oh, I understand," he looked disappointed.

"But, I guess a peak won't hurt."

She pulled off her black blazer, placed it through her open car window, and swung it to the passenger's seat.

"Come this way," he led her to a beautiful creek with clear water streaming over gray rocks. The trees were a bright lush green. Beyond the creek were dogwood trees, the beautiful white bracts fell beautifully to the ground like snow. A beautiful golden ray of sunlight shined down in between the two center dogwood trees and gave the sight a majestic feel. Laila took a deep breath, taking in the fresh air. She felt at ease. The sounds of birds chirping always calmed her. She looked up and saw a blue jay flying from tree to tree.

"Watch your step," Laila stumbled; Quinton held her hand as they stepped over the larger rocks. They began walking along the stream.

"So what do you do again?"

"Oh, I'm an Advertising Manager."

"Really? That's sounds like fun."

"Oh, it has been. I have been with Hearst & Mitchell for about four years now. Recently, they've been on that bullshit though."

"What happened?"

"Well, James Hearst runs the company. He oversees the daily activities of everyone from top level management down to the interns. He knows each of us by face and name. Mitchell, on the other hand, is like a silent partner. He sits on his fat ass and collects his checks. Hearst is in the process of opening about three more firms in three different states. They decided to downsize our firm,"

"Why?"

"Well, since we're the best advertising firm in the state, they wanted to get rid of the weak links, and let the qualified employees take on more responsibilities. So, we were finally able to meet Mitchell and he was there for one purpose and one purpose only, to fire some asses. He told me I was fired just so he can give my job to his golf buddy's daughter who just finished college. I acted a damn fool and he even got security to take me out. The directors tried to talk to him, but he wouldn't hear any of it. So, there I was, without a job, and Melanie threatening to leave my ass."

"Wow,"

"I sat at home for seven days, the longest I've ever been without a job. Then, Hearst came back and immediately called, begging me to come back. I had brought them more clients than anybody and was kicked in the ass. I mean that was embarrassing to be dragged out; it took all of my pride. I told him as long as Mitchell was there, I want no part of Hearst & Mitchell. He offered me a raise and all kind of perks, I told him I'll think about it. So, he told me to take my vacation and it's full-paid. We are entitled to three one-week vacations and I'm taking all of mine back-to-back right now. Mitchell can't do a damn thing about it because I can take all of their clients and open my own firm."

"That is a shame and very unfair of Mitchell," Laila paused, "so why was Melanie threatening to leave you?"

"Oh, we were having some issues. She was just stressin' about planning for the wedding and honeymoon. We're straight now though,"

"Oh."

"So you work at the bank?"

"Yeah, similar to what you just said, I have dual responsibilities too."

"Oh really?"

"Yes, I am a loan officer and Director of Diversity Relations."

"Oooo, sounds good. What's that?"

She giggled, "I basically accept or reject loan applications and assist in hiring multi-cultural people and make sure that their rights are being protected."

"Okay, so you and Alonzo both majored in Banking and Finance."

"Oh really?"

"Yeah, he's a Financial Advisor."

"Oh okay," she said dryly.

He smiled, "You still don't care much for Alonzo, do you?"

"Uh no,"

He laughed to himself.

"You got hot with me the other night."

"Yeah, I don't like to be disrespected."

"Oh well, I didn't mean to honestly. It wasn't my intention."

"Okay,"

"So what do you think about me and Melanie?"

"Um, it was unexpected news."

"Yeah, my boys were shocked too… as much as you

and I used to hang out."

"Ummm huh," Laila said through tight lips.

"I can tell you're uncomfortable with us."

"I mean I would have been comfortable if you two would have given me a heads up two years ago. It would have taken some time to get used to it."

"Oh, well that's all on Melanie, keeping her girls out of the loop."

"Yea and now, this gets sprung on me and I have to be maid of honor."

He studied her eyes. "You still have feelings for me, don't you? You can tell me. I promise I won't tell."

"I – I don't know. We haven't seen each other in years, so I don't even know you now just the eighteen-year-old that I dreamed about being with."

He smiled. "Yeah, I used to dream about you too."

She took a deep breath and then realized the conversation was going in the wrong direction.

"Well, Quinton this is a beautiful location, but I have to go to work now."

"Alright, let me walk you back to your car," they started making their way through the woods.

"You always could understand beauty. You remember when we went on that senior trip. You were amazed to see nature at its best on top of that mountain. Marla hated it. Now, you're here taking in the beauty of this stream."

"And beautiful *woods*." Laila chuckled.

"I can't believe Melanie called this place the woods like she's never lived in the country before. She keep doing me like this and we gon' be getting married right here with the preacher standing in the bed of an old red pickup truck."

"Oh, now that would kill her." Laila laughed.

"Laila, thank you for telling me Melanie couldn't make it. Even though she asked you to, you still came out of the kindness of your own heart. That just shows me you're being a good friend to me already."

He placed his hand on hers. Laila nervously look down at their hands, then back at him.

"And Laila please convince your friend that this is the best place to take our post-wedding pictures."

"I will try my best."

"For me to be an advertiser, I can't sell that woman a thing."

"That's because she's stubborn. It's her way or the highway."

"I know it," he agreed.

They stared at each other and Laila looked away. She cleared her throat, "So um, I'll see you at the wedding rehearsal."

He was in a daze. "Uh yeah," he managed to say.

Laila rushed to get in her car and quickly press the ignition button.

"You drive safely now Laila,"

"And you be careful here in these *woods*."

They smiled at each other and he watched her as she pulled out and drove away.

CHAPTER 10

It was 12:02, and Laila would normally be tucked away in bed. She was sitting alone, pouring a glass of wine, at her dinner table. Her normal nightcap was not enough to bring her slumber. The full bottle of Merlot had tapered to half in a matter of seconds. She rested her elbow on the table and placed her hand to her head, rubbing her temple. She sighed, thoughts of Quinton and Melanie would not leave her mind.

I keep trying to get over him, but somehow I end up with him whether it's in a cozy bathroom, at a romantic stream . . . I can't even fathom the fact that I actually stand in church and watch the man I've always wanted practice his vows with my best friend!

She heard a knock at her door.

"Who is bothering me at this hour?"

She silently hoped that it wasn't Melanie. Maybe it was Kecia. She called Laila earlier complaining about Leonard and that she planned on spending the night at her mother's house. Laila grabbed her glass, quickly finished her wine, and rushed to the door. She looked through the peephole and quickly opened the door.

"Quinton?"

What is he doing here?

"I just had to see you," he said anxiously. Laila was confused; she looked past him.

"Where did you come from?" she looked at him, "Where is your car? Where's Melanie?"

"Melanie is at her aunt's place, and I walked from my mother's house. I didn't know you lived so close."

She stared at him. She could tell he was beating around the bush.

"Yep, my bachelor party is going on right now as we speak," he said in a daze.

"So what are you doing here?" she finally asked.

"I just couldn't stop thinking about you so I decided to walk over."

"From your bachelor party?" she looked him in his teary red eyes. "Have you been drinking?"

"Um no," he lied and invited himself in. Laila rushed to the door, looked out to see if anyone saw him, closed the door and turned the lock. She turned around to find Quinton, sitting on the arm of her white sofa, gazing at her.

"Quinton, what's wrong?"

"It has been years since we graduated from high school, and um, I can't stop thinking about you."

"*You* can't stop thinking about *me*? Well, I know you weren't thinking of me when you got involved with Melanie."

"What? Laila, you were the first person I asked about when I saw her. She kept telling me about your fiancé so I figured since we both lived in different states anyway, why should I try to ruin a good thing?"

"Well, she lied because I've never been engaged and I haven't even had a serious relationship in years."

"Really? Damn," he shook his head and blew his breath. "Why couldn't I have seen you just once? Then, I could have told you face-to-face how I felt…that I'm in love with you."

Laila frowned and crossed her arms, "Well, it's too late

to hear about your *feelings*? You're getting married."

He was lost in thought. "Damn, things were much easier in high school. You could drop a girl just like that," he snapped his fingers, "when the one you've always wanted finally comes around."

"Well, I wanted to be with you back then, and you wouldn't drop Marla Gomillion."

"No, *you* didn't drop that pretty boy for me," he said referring to her ex, Deon, "I didn't care about Marla."

She shook her head. "Tell that to someone who doesn't know any better."

Laila wrinkled her brows, *What? He is lying, if not to me, then to himself.*

He began to look around.

"So this is your house. You've done very well for yourself."

He walked down the hall, opening doors, and peeping into every room. When he reached her room, he walked right in. The room was dimly lit by a lamp on her nightstand. She followed him and watched as he plopped down on her bed and ran his hands across the soft, cool plush white comforter.

"This feels so damn good. Now, I need one like this. Where you get this from?"

Laila sat beside him and ignored his question.

Is this real? Is the man of my dreams sitting in my bedroom? Why now? Why after he proposed to my best friend? What is he thinking? Now he's sitting here like everything is okay?

"Quinton, how can you just drop a bombshell on me, then walk around my house like it's no big deal? What were you hoping to accomplish?"

"I don't know. Maybe get closure."

"Closure? You want closure, huh? How can *I* get closure when I've wanted you for so long? How can I move on knowing that Melanie didn't want us together in the first place?"

A tear ran down her cheek, and her heart felt heavy.

"How can we possibly find closure?"

She desperately searched his eyes for the answer. He wiped her tears away and caressed her cheek.

"I love you and you will always be that beautiful innocent girl I could never get," he sighed and licked his lips, "And now that you're all grown up, you are even more beautiful. Your eyes are entrancing, and your lips are still so damn enticing. I just can't help bu-"

He slowly came closer and kissed her, a short and sweet kiss. They looked at each other and their lips met once again. His kisses were just how she remembered. From short rapid kisses to a long French kiss, their eyes met once again. They both knew what they were doing was wrong, but they had reached the point of no return. They held onto each other tightly, still passionately locking lips. Laila didn't want to let go. He was finally where he was always supposed to be…with her.

"Let me have you," he looked deeply into her eyes and bit his bottom lip, "…just this once."

She had been waiting eight years for him to find her and tell her that he wanted her. She was drawn by him and in a trance, she nodded.

Quinton circled her with pure admiration in his eyes, then came behind her and placed his hands on her shoulders. It was such a familiar feeling to Laila. Her chest began to rise and fall as she panted heavily. He gently massaged her and she felt at ease. She exhaled. He ran his fingers down her arms. Then, pressed his lips against her neck and then her right shoulder. She leaned back into him. She could feel him rise against her backside. She smiled in delight. He whispered in ear, "Just like old times huh?"

She turned to face him and pressed her lips against his as he ran his fingers through her curls. Laila tried to unbuckle his pants, but couldn't unlatch them. They both looked down and bumped heads.

"Ow," they both said as they held their heads.

"My bad, I got it," Quinton said as he unbuckled his black pants.

As he began to undress himself, Laila sat back in delight like a young girl exploring the male anatomy for the first time. She unclothed herself until she was completely nude. She inched back on the bed and grabbed one of the condoms that Gia had bought her as a joke. She gave it to him after he took off his blue boxers. She admired his bare body. It was the first time she had ever seen him fully exposed. She stared at his abdomen. His six-pack that he had when he was 18 had disappeared. She could probably pinch the skin on his stomach now. But, she looked down and stared in amazement at his member.

He stared at her and began breathing heavily. His breath smelled of beer yet his mouth tasted of mint. Laila closed her eyes and replayed the day they were alone in his bedroom when they were teenagers. It felt like an old movie that had been placed on pause for so many years, and now, they were about to finally get a chance to experience the next scene. All she needed was that Fuchsia that he had placed in her hair.

I knew it. Quinton is mine.

He slowly pulled the condom over his throbbing head. He looked at her intensely and climbed on top of her. They kissed as he felt his way to her most intimate place. He slowly eased in with a struggle.

"Aw shit," he said aloud as he slowly inched his way through her tight walls. Once he was fully submerged in her, he began to give her soft, smooth strokes.

He moaned at how narrow she was. It felt like he was taking her virginity... like he had always wanted to in high school. He continued his pulsating struggle until he was completely inside of her.

She couldn't stop herself from smiling. It had been a long time since she had sex with a man she actually wanted. Her entire body felt calm and relaxed as Quinton took his time and made love to her.

She purred, closed her eyes, and bit her bottom lip. He took his time with each stroke as if he wanted to savor every moment.

"Aw, Laila this feels so good," Quinton moaned. Laila squeezed her walls, fully enveloping him. His eyes grew wide and his mouth dropped. Then, he climaxed and let out a deep, gratifying sigh. Laila didn't want it to end but she knew he had to get back to his bachelor party before anyone noticed he was gone. Quinton collapsed on top of her. She wrapped her arms around him, looked up at the ceiling, reveling in knowing that she and the man she always wanted were finally one.

CHAPTER 11

Bang! Bang!

Laila awoke to a knock on her door.

"Laila!" she heard Melanie call from outside.

"Oh shit!" she fell out of the bed with her sheet wrapped around her. Her heart was beating rapidly and she felt dizzy. She shook her head, so she could become alert. She quickly got up and shoved Quinton, but he wouldn't budge.

"Melanie's outside. You have to get out of here," she whispered. He began to come to. "If she finds out you're here, she's going to kick my ass."

"Melanie?" He jumped out of the bed and quickly put on his clothes.

"How do I get out of here?"

Laila looked out of the window.

"Why do the neighbors have to be out so early?" she groaned.

Her phone rang. She picked it up off the floor and saw Melanie's picture on her screen.

"It's her, shhh..." Laila's head began to throb, "Hello?"

"Hey girl, don't you hear me knocking out here? I need

your help with the wedding."

"Oh, I'm tired. We can meet later on."

"Oh no, Ms. Lady. It is your duty as maid of honor to make sure everything goes on without a hitch."

She sighed, "Well, you can-"

"Laila, you're not getting rid of me that easily, so come on," she coaxed, "I know where you hide your extra key."

Thank God she didn't use it.

"Remind me to move it," she sighed, "Just wait, I'll be right out."

She quickly ended the call and threw her cell on the bed. She rushed over to her door and picked a blue satin robe from her collection of Chinese pattern robes.

Uh, I have to wash my robes. The red and green are the only two left now.

She looked at Quinton.

"Do not turn your phone on for any reason," she ordered him. She closed the door behind her and rushed down the hall. She tied her robe as she walked across the living room.

Once she reached the door, she took a deep breath, exhaled, and opened the door.

"Finally," she looked at Laila's unruly hair, "Did I catch you at a bad time?" She walked past her.

"Yes, a very bad time."

"Oh, I'm sorry. I don't like to interrupt anyone's beauty sleep, but my wedding is right around the corner and I just want everything to be perfect."

"Okay, just let me get ready and clean up a bit."

She rushed into the dining room and Melanie followed. She picked up her wine glass and wine bottle from the table and placed them on the kitchen counter. She poured herself a glass of water and popped two aspirins in her mouth.

"You were drinking last night?"

Laila drank the whole glass of water and let out a sigh. "Yes, I was. Had a nightcap or two?"

"Or two? This wine bottle is almost empty," Melanie smiled, "Could it be that two people were in here drinking last night?"

"What?" Laila's head panged again and she rubbed it with one hand.

"Could it be that the second glass is sitting by your nightstand?"

"Melanie, you're not making any sense," she started washing her glass nervously.

"Laila, you have a certain glow this morning and look at your hair," Melanie said. Laila walked pass her toward the dining table, then turned and looked at her.

"What's this?"

"Huh? What's what?" her eyes grew wide.

"This," she started digging through her friend's hair and pulled out a piece of a condom wrapper.

Laila gasped, "Give me that."

"You got some last night, didn't you?"

She could hear Gia say in her head, *Damn bitch, the golden wrapper wasn't a good enough clue for your ass.* She remained quiet.

Melanie sniffed, "Is he still here?"

Laila paused in fear.

"Huh?" she asked, "Oh, yeah. He-he-he's resting."

"Hmm… Curve. Quinton wears the same cologne. I love it because when he leaves the room it lingers for the longest time."

"Yes, gotta love the Curve," she said nervously.

"So um,"

"Melanie," she warned. "I'd like to keep my relationships private."

"Aw come on. Don't hold out on me. We once told each other everything. Who is he? Do I know him?"

I know she did not just tell me that when she's been dating Quinton for years and springs a wedding on everyone. Who's really been holding out and hiding everything?

Laila tried to come up with a *good lie*, so she closed her

eyes, held her breath, exhaled and the words began to flow.

"Melanie, we are in the beginning stages of the relationship. I don't want to introduce him to the important people in my life right now until I know we are going to take our relationship further."

Hmmm, Melanie's method of lying actually works.

"Oh okay, you can't even reveal his name?"

"No."

"But I thought you were going through a celibacy phase."

"Well, I guess it ended last night," she said coyly. Melanie smiled and shook her head.

"Damn girl, I bet you wore him out. I'm going to let you handle *business* and then you can meet me at the hotel for lunch."

"Yes, that sounds great."

"Okay. Love you girl."

She walked out. Laila rushed and locked the door behind her. She walked towards the hall and collapsed against the wall, sighing in relief.

***

Alonzo was driving around in the neighborhood looking at his surroundings. He was bobbing his head listening to R. Kelly's "Get Dirty." Then he parked along the right shoulder of the main highway and left the engine of his silver Range Rover running. Quinton appeared within the greenery. His white undershirt was wrinkled and black dress pants were unzipped. He was holding his balled up shirt in one hand while he was fighting his way through the bushes with the other. A bush smacked him in the face. Alonzo smirked, sighed, and then shook his head. He was typically the one who would be involved in such a predicament. Now, that it was Quinton; he was not impressed. Quinton hopped in the SUV, threw his shirt on the backseat, and quickly zipped his pants up.

"I appreciate this, man."

Alonzo shook his head, looked in his rearview mirror, and pulled out onto the street. He turned the volume down on his satellite radio and there was complete silence.

"What are you doing, man?"

"It was nothing, just a one-time ordeal."

Alonzo shook his head. "If it was Marla Gomillion, I would have understood. But Laila of all people? You know how close she and Melanie are."

"Yeah, I know man."

"I know you two played this game of cat and mouse in high school, but we're in the big leagues now. You're about to get married. That's major, and definitely something that shouldn't be taken lightly," he bit his bottom lip and sighed, "Both of our parents' marriages ended in divorce only because our fathers cheated. You of all people should want to get it right the first time…I don't know about you, but I don't want to end up like my father."

"Yeah, you're right."

"Jamal, Al, and even Chuck are cheating on their wives. Don't you see what it's doing to their lives? Their kids' lives. They shouldn't have made that leap across the threshold if they were going to do the same old thing they did when they were single. That's the way I see it."

"I know, man," Quinton said, "I love Melanie. I wouldn't have asked her to marry me if I didn't think we had a future together."

"Then, why are you creeping with her best friend with the wedding around the corner?"

Quinton shrugged and sighed, and then he looked at Alonzo suspiciously. He knew if he had spent the night with any woman but Laila, Alonzo would have never given him that lecture, chastising his actions. He would be singing his praises and telling Quinton he was the man.

Alonzo stopped at the four-way intersection and looked at Quinton.

"I know you wanted Laila back then, we all did, but

this was not the time to finally get her," he continued.

"Come on man. I'm tired. I just want to lie down."

Alonzo watched as two cars passed through. Then, the road was clear, but he didn't move. "So how was it?"

Quinton chuckled. "Now, that sounds more like you. Just drive man and turn the radio to that Jamie Foxx station."

"Alright, I see how you wanna be. I'll find out one way or the other."

CHAPTER 12

Laila took a deep breath. It was a close call. Melanie almost caught her and Quinton. She had come into work late for the first time and she had been nervous the entire morning. It was time for her break and she hated that she even agreed to have lunch with Melanie. She pulled up at the Town Bakery; Melanie had texted her earlier and changed their lunch to the restaurant on the square, The Town Bakery. When the girls were in high school, they would go get a burger, fries, and milkshake from the bakery. They would also split a small chocolate cake. So, she was delighted when Melanie wanted to eat at their old hangout spot instead of the hotel.

As she approached the bakery, she noticed Melanie waiting for her on the sidewalk.

"I'm sorry I disturbed you this morning and now your lunch break."

"Oh, it's fine."

"I'm glad you could come. Carol is getting on my last nerves."

"Really?"

"Yes, she blatantly disrespected me. She has a ten by fourteen prom picture of Quinton and Marla hanging on her living room wall. She just doesn't know once our wedding portraits arrive, every high school photo of him and her is coming down. I do not care what she has to say about it."

"You're still having the wedding?" Laila asked, then cleared her throat, "...rehearsal um...tomorrow?"

"Yes, Carol insisted on us having another rehearsal, so she could see it. She has to approve everything, what she doesn't know is the final say lies with me."

Wow, she has to worry about Mrs. Harris, Marla, and ... and, Laila tried to think of someone else and remembered, *me? Oh no! What have I done? Okay, you can do this. Just focus on your comfort, food.*

Laila sighed, "I'm glad we're having lunch here. I'm craving some meat...a steak or maybe their famous bacon Swiss double cheeseburger. I haven't had that in years."

"Oh no, darling. We're here to cake-taste for the reception, silly," she smiled and opened the door to the bakery and Laila rolled her eyes as she followed behind her friend.

Soon, they were sitting at a table with various slices of cakes on their plates. Melanie had a dime-sized piece of cake on her fork and placed the cake in her mouth. Laila was staring at her plate and holding her fork, playing around with a piece. She couldn't bring herself to look Melanie in the eyes.

"Laila, are you okay?"

Laila quickly looked up, "Yes, yes, I'm fine. Why wouldn't I be?"

"You've been quiet since I stopped by your place. Is something wrong?"

She spoke rapidly, "Um no, why? You think something is wrong? Because I can assure you nothing is going on..." her eyes grew big, "With me, with me." With a nervous sigh, she added, "Nothing's wrong with me."

"Okay, okay. Calm down. It may be my fault since I practically dragged you away from your hot guy friend."

"Oh no… Him? He's um…real busy…not planning on seeing him today… Yes, he has a big day planned…today."

"Oh okay," she tasted another piece of cake, "Um, now this is the best buttercream frosting I've ever tasted. I wanted a chocolate torte with a raspberry center, covered in a silky ribbon of French vanilla frosting, but," she exhaled, "Quinton hates raspberries and claims his guests prefer his aunt's pound cake. Can you believe it? A pound cake for a wedding? So, that's why we're here at The Town Bakery, making it as simple as possible for the Bolton-Harris side even though it's *my* wedding."

Laila rolled her eyes and said sarcastically, "Yea, I bet the Whitman-Taylor side would appreciate a good tort."

Hmm, I've never met any of them except her Aunt Judy.

"Hi, baby. I'm sorry I'm late," Quinton approached them. Laila's heart began to race. They briefly looked at each other and their eyes quickly darted away. Melanie stood up to greet him, and Laila started picking up pieces of cake and eating them.

"Where have you been? I've been calling you all morning?"

"Oh, you know the bachelor party…I had too much to drink and I've just been sleeping it off."

"Oh, I was beginning to think you had run off with a stripper," she joked.

Laila quickly drank a full glass of water and wiped her mouth with a napkin.

"Naw, never that. No one can keep me from you."

What? Those words sent a sharp, cold pain through her body.

"Aw, I've missed you,"

They hugged and Melanie tried to kiss him, but he turned away and her lips landed on his cheek. Then, she turned his face to hers and kissed him. Laila just stared in shock and pain as he stood there and disrespected her and their night together. Melanie turned away to talk to the baker. Quinton quickly looked at Laila. She was shaking her head with tears in her eyes. She quickly got up.

"Laila, wait," he said in a low voice and she rushed out of the door.

"Hey, where's Laila?"

"Oh she said um…she was running late," he lied.

"Oh yea, she had to get back to work. Come on, darling. See which cake you like the best out of *my* favorite selections."

CHAPTER 13

It had been a while since Laila had went to the store, so she decided to drop by Wal-Mart after work to get groceries and toiletries. Her mind was a million miles away. It had been hard to concentrate. Her mind had been on Quinton the whole day. She hadn't been alone with him since the morning he snuck out of her bathroom window. Then, she had to smile in Melanie's face and pretend like everything was okay and then, watch them kiss. It was Marla Gomillion all over again; she should have known Quinton hadn't changed. All through high school, she had to sneak around with Quinton so Marla wouldn't find out. Now, it's Melanie. Same situation. Different woman. Same result. Laila doesn't get the man in the end. She shook her head.

She noticed two old men were sitting on the bench gawking at her in her beige and black houndstooth quarter-length sleeved jacket, black skirt, and beige pumps. She spoke to the greeter, Ms. Helen, a skinny black woman in her late fifties with a short honey-blonde pixie cut.

"Hey, baby. You workin' that suit girl."

"Thank you, Ms. Helen."

"Aw, they worked you hard at that bank today, didn't

they?"

"Yes, ma'am."

"I knew it. It's written all over your face," she smiled. "Don't worry, baby. It's all gonna pay off. You just wait and see baby. You just wait and see."

"Thanks, Ms. Helen," Laila forced a smile.

She went to the cart corral to find a cart already pulled out. She was relieved that she didn't have to struggle with pulling the carts apart as she always fought with them. She pulled a disinfectant wipe from the display and wiped the handle of her cart, and tossed it in the waste basket. She decided to make her way to the produce section to get some fruit. She had a taste for strawberries. After she spent thirty minutes in the food section, she decided to make her way to the other side of the supercenter to get deodorant and body wash. As she passed the checkout aisles in the front, she noticed Quinton and his mom walking towards the jewelry counter. She froze in her steps. She would have to walk by him, but she couldn't face him at least not today.

"So what you think about this, baby?" his mother pointed at a bracelet in the glass counter. He looked up at Laila in surprise.

Laila's heart began to pound once again and she began to breathe heavily. She looked like a deer caught in headlights.

"Baby?" Carol looked at him and followed his gaze. Laila shyly waved at them and they waved back. Carol started looking back at Quinton who was still staring.

Laila could feel another pair of eyes on her from her right down checkout aisle #5. She gazed down to see Marla Gomillion at the register, sneering at her, shaking her head, and laughing to herself as she scanned her only customer's groceries.

Well, she obviously saw Quinton too.

Laila rolled her eyes, then turned her cart around and quickly made her way to the back of the store. Laila's heart was still pounding.

How can I face him? How can I stand there behind Melanie after we made love? After we professed our love?

Laila exhaled.

Well, he made his decision. He decided to go on with the wedding, so that's that.

Laila turned the corner as she placed a bulk of tissue in her cart, and Quinton was standing on the aisle. Laila jumped and held her chest; her heart raced once more.

"Laila?"

"Quinton, you frightened me." she said fiddling with her pearl necklace.

"Oh, I'm sorry…um," he licked his lips, "I know you're probably wondering why I haven't called…"

Laila looked at him strangely. He actually thought she was sitting around waiting for a call when she knew that he was spending time with Melanie and planning a wedding that is still on. Besides, she didn't even give him her phone number.

"…well um…came over," he corrected himself.

"Actually, no I wasn't wondering any of that."

"Laila, you just seemed so hurt when you saw Melanie and I together, so I-"

"Look," she interrupted, "I'm a big girl, Quinton"

"You're – You're not confused?"

"Confused? What is there to be confused about?"

He raised his brows in shock that she was speaking to him with an attitude.

She continued, "You were having cold feet and you saw me…had your way with me and that's that. I was your last conquest, soirée or whatever it's called, so now you can get married."

"No, it's not like that."

She smirked, "I just want this wedding to hurry up and come, so I can go back to living my life the way it was,"

"Laila, I li-"

"Hey, I have to go, so see you at the wedding

rehearsal."

She pushed her cart past him.

"So um?" he turned and looked at her, "Thi- this is going to stay between us?"

"Let's be clear, I don't spread my personal business, so who can *I* possibly tell?"

CHAPTER 14

"You did what?" Kecia asked in shock.

"Oh my damn!" Gia said

Laila and her two friends had decided to dine at the new Lakefront Grill for lunch. They were sitting at a table on a platform overlooking the lake. The tables by them were empty, but the other tables were filled with people enjoying their meal.

"Girl, you heard her. She slept with Quinton."

"Shhh," Laila said looking around.

"When did this happen?"

"A few days ago," she said.

"So how was it?"

"Don't answer that," Kecia interjected, "I know Melanie did you wrong, but you didn't have to stoop to her level. Laila, she is about to marry that man."

"I know, I know. I just don't know what came over me."

"I have to give it to you. I didn't think you had it in you... That's what Melanie gets for doing her dirty deeds."

"Gia, this is nothing to be patting her on the back for."

"Oh yes it is." Gia patted Laila's back. "Job well done." Laila cut her eyes at Gia.

"Dang Gia, what kind of friend are you? It's a shame you two can do this to your best friend. It makes me wonder what kind of friend you are to me," she got up.

"Melanie ain't never been our best friend." Gia said.

"Kecia, don't leave," Laila said.

"I ain't leaving. I'm going to the restroom and wondering what you have turned into," she walked off.

"Kecia."

"Let her go. She'll come around. She's just having male problems her damn self. So what now?"

"I guess nothing, but from that night, I know Quinton would rather be with me than her."

"Oh okay. So you're getting revenge on Melanie by getting your man back. I think I like the new you."

Gia and Laila discussed Kecia and her man. Kecia finally came back to sit down.

"I'm hungry. These three small meals a day are killing me."

"Girl, eat and stop worrying about losing weight."

Melanie appeared wearing a white high-waist skirt, and a sleeveless dull blue top with her white cashmere sweater resting on her back with the sleeves tied in the front. She was holding a white clutch in her hand. Melanie reeked heavily of bourgeois that day. As Laila looked at her, she could feel a knot in her throat, her stomach panged, and anxiety slowly eased in. As she made her way to the table, her engagement ring glared in Laila's eyes almost blinding her. Laila frowned as she squinted her eyes. The engagement ring. She hadn't noticed it before. Melanie made no mention of it at the barbecue or any of their gatherings. She didn't flaunt it like most gushing bride-to-bes typically do. That day, Laila felt as if she had a flashlight directed at her by an usher at a movie theatre. Maybe, in a strange way, the ring was shining a light on Laila and Quinton's indiscretion. "Okay girls, what did I miss?" Melanie sat down. The girls looked at each other strangely. Gia began to speak in a British accent.

"We were discussing the ancient ruins of the Mayan civilization."

"Really, I'm impressed. You typically discuss how men are 'so damn fine.'"

"Well, my tastes have changed since you've been gone. I'm more refined."

Kecia gave her a look. A handsome man passed by, and the girls looked at him.

"Umm . . . now if you'll excuse me, I'm about to make him my baby daddy."

She got up, whipped her hair back, and switched her hips as she walked toward him.

"Get him girl."

"I see Gia is still crazy."

"Yeah, pretty much."

"Woo, I am tired. I was just on the phone with the caterer, and I don't know whether to pick between the filet mignon and the Cornish hen."

"How about chicken or fish? Ooo, I would eat both of them right now if I could."

"You can," Laila said.

"Aw, Laila told me you were on a diet."

"Oh, she did, huh?" she glared at Laila who lowered her head. Kecia hated for Melanie to know any of her personal issues.

"Personally, I think you're beautiful just the way you are."

Kecia was surprised and touched. "Well, thank you Melanie."

"Not all women look right skinny," she added to her previous statement.

"So that's why I shouldn't lose weight? Because *you* don't think I would look right?"

Laila jumped in before they started fussing. She knew how Kecia would react to anyone who slammed her weight. She could see how the argument would play out. Kecia would tell off Melanie in a long-winded, profanity-filled decree and then finish it off by saying, *that's why Laila's fucking your man*.

"It's not about how you look. It's about how you feel, so Kecia do whatever makes you happy."

"Thank you, Laila."

With her elbow on the table and chin resting on her hand, Melanie asked, "So Kecia, how is your boyfriend?"

"He's okay. He's getting ready to go on a business trip."

Gia sat back down. "Four minutes, a new record. I didn't have to say one word. He looked at me and just started begging for my number and a date. He just couldn't resist all of this here."

"All of what?" Kecia asked.

"So you got jokes. Jasper and I are going out tonight."

"I'm not mad at you."

"Aw damn, I'm closing the shop tonight."

Melanie never stopped looking at Kecia. "So, Kecia what does your boyfriend do for a living?"

"Oh, he's a car salesman."

"A car salesman?"

"That's what I said."

"But I didn't think car salesmen went on business trips."

"Well, mine does."

"So where did he say he was going?"

"He is going to Arkansas to the Ford plant, so he can check on a shipment of cars."

Gia asked, "So what is he gon' do? Follow the cars down here?"

Kecia clenched her teeth. "I don't know. They had a problem with the shipment and his boss entrusted him to go fix it. End of story."

"I don't know, Kecia. That doesn't sound right," Laila added.

"It doesn't," Melanie agreed.

"Nuh uh," Gia said.

"Do any of you hefas know anything about cars and their production? I didn't think so. So you hefas stay out of my business."

"Okay, okay." Melanie said.

"I'm sorry," Laila said.

"Actually we were in *his* business," Gia said.

Kecia cut her eyes at her.

"I'm just saying," Gia held up her hands.

"You girls will never change." Melanie smiled, "Laila, you're awful quiet."

"Yeah Laila. You are. Anything on your mind?" Kecia asked.

"No, I'm just tired."

"From all of the sex you've been having?" Melanie smiled.

"What?" Gia asked.

"Tell me. Who is the mystery man?" Melanie said.

"Oh, I'm not telling anyone."

"Why keep it a secret unless you have something to hide?" Kecia asked.

"Yeah, why won't you tell us?" Melanie looked suspicious.

Gia came to Laila's defense. "Hey y'all, leave the woman alone. Like Kecia was just preaching, it's her business."

"Thank you, Gia."

"You know I got your back girl."

"You girls better have mine on my wedding day because I am going to need all of the help I can get. I want my wedding to be absolutely flawless."

Kecia looked at Laila. "How could it ever be flawed?"

She sank down in her chair.

***

Quinton, Alonzo, Taaz, and David were playing basketball with two of their friends, Jamal and Al in front of Carol's garage. They had just finished a game of three-on-three and were taking a break.

"Man, there are some fine ladies on the girls' side," Jamal said referring to the bridal party.

"Um… that Laila," David said. Alonzo and Quinton looked at each other. Alonzo raised his brows and Quinton scratched his head.

"Naw, Gia," Al said.

"Shoot, everyone but Kecia," Taaz pointed out.

Alonzo shook his head. "Man, why do you still have it in for Kecia?"

"Yeah, y'all been at it since like the third grade, man," David said.

"I just don't like that girl. Just to think of her makes me . . . ugh," he shivered.

Quinton interceded. "You've always talked about Kecia's size, but I hope you know size doesn't matter."

"What they say? Mo' cushion for the pushin'," Al said as he high-fived Jamal. The guys all started laughing and making small banter.

"Naw, naw. It ain't about the physical." Alonzo said, "You've got to see a plus-sized woman like you would any other woman. It ain't no difference to me; it's women's attitudes that get me."

"My mother is a beautiful plus-sized woman. She always says every layer she has makes her the intelligent strong courageous woman she is today. She said rip away her layers and you rip away her identity. I would never want my mom to change."

"Ain't we supposed to be playing ball? I didn't know we was on the damn Dr. Phil show? Man, y'all trippin' for real."

"Naw, you are."

"Hey, I ain't got a problem with Kecia or anybody else's size."

"Right," Quinton smirked as he shot the ball and made the basket. Alonzo threw the ball back to him.

"Now Q, you remember when I tried to get with your momma in high school." Taaz looked off and shivered.

"Uh, she was so fine until I just wanted to-"

"Ah!" he looked at Taaz, "If you finish that statement, I'ma kick your ass." He shot the ball and made it once again.

"I'm just saying man," he started thinking. Then, he bit his bottom lip, "Um, she hasn't even aged since high school. She got that short jet black hair. She be wearing those nice ass clothes, jewelry, and heels. And she just smell so damn good and all soft and warm. It's just like snuggling with a pillow fresh out the *dryer*." Everyone, but Quinton, laughed at his silliness. Quinton hit him in the stomach with the ball. Alonzo motioned for Taaz to throw him the ball.

"I ain't gone lie man. Your momma do smell good," David said.

"Yeah, that's true," Alonzo agreed as he shot the ball and missed.

Everyone else nodded in agreement. Taaz retrieved the ball. Quinton defiantly looked at them.

"Ah! Y'all better get off my momma!"

Taaz looked at Quinton. "Get off her? Man, I wish I was on her," he started hunching the ball. Quinton rushed at him, and they start tussling. Everyone crowded around them, trying to pull Quinton away from Taaz. Carol pulled up in her wine-colored Nissan Altima. Everyone froze in their tracks and stared at her. Quinton had Taaz in a head lock.

"Hey Ms. Harris," all the guys said to his mom.

"Hey boys," she smiled, then looked at her son, "Quinton, what are you doing to Taaz?"

"Oh nothing, Ma. We- We were just playing."

Quinton released Taaz, and Taaz rushed over to help Carol out of her car.

"Hey baby," he said and she shook her head.

"Hey Taaz," he kissed her on the cheek.

"Let me help you with your groceries."

"Well, that's very nice of you," she said. Taaz looked at

Quinton and stuck out his tongue.

Alonzo shook his head. "I swear this is high school all over again."

CHAPTER 15

Gia was sweeping the floor of her work station. She placed the broom in the storage closet and straightened a few chairs in the waiting area. She slowly made her way to the front door. Just as she changed her sign to "closed," Marla appeared at the door.

"We're closed."

"Gia, please I just got off. I've been working every day this week. This is the only time I can get my hair done. Please Gia," she sighed and reluctantly opened the door.

"Come on."

"Thank you."

"You better be glad I was closing the shop tonight 'cuz those other hefas would have left you out there."

"Yeah, I know."

Gia reached her station and motioned for Marla to sit in the styling chair. She obeyed.

"What you want done?"

"Oh, just a shampoo and style."

"Okay, you want your hair curled?"

"Yeah," Gia plugged up her curling base, and found her small curlers and stuck them in. Then, she reached in her drawer and pulled out her business card.

"Here's my card," Marla took it and looked at it, "and on that card are the days in which I have after hours appointments. So call me and we'll get a slot just for you the next time, okay?"

"Okay." Gia placed a black cover over Marla.

"So how is your mother doing?"

"She's about the same."

"It has to be pretty hard to work, take care of your mother, and help your sister with those bad ass kids of hers," she squirted shampoo in her hand and applied it to Marla's head.

"Yeah, I rarely have time for myself. Momma constantly tells me to live my life and put her in a home, but I just wouldn't feel right doing it. You know in some cultures, taking care of your parents is top priority. It is frowned upon if you put them off on someone else."

Still massaging the shampoo into Marla's scalp, "Well, that's what she wants. She's lived her life, now she wants you to live yours."

"She says I need to go out more and find love...whatever that means."

"She's right, girl...everybody needs a good man to be up against at night," Gia said, "Now, come on to the sink." Marla sat in the chair against the sink and leaned back. Gia picked up the sprayer and cut on the water. She tested the temperature on her hand, then she started rinsing Marla's hair. Marla closed her eyes.

"Ooo, you know who you should get back with?"

"Who?"

"Quinton."

"Quinton?" She opened her eyes. "Quinton Harris? You can't be serious."

"Yeah, I know he's marrying Melanie, but that ho don't deserve him. Someone needs to teach her that she can't have everything."

"I know that's right. I saw her at the store and she was looking down on me just because I'm a cashier."

"Uh, she ain't even working. Talking about she's a 'buyer for a boutique.' Then, why the hell are we buying our own damn bridesmaid's dresses and she's trying on dresses in this country ass town's shop?"

"A buyer for a boutique? That's 'bout the oldest made up job in the unemployment handbook."

"I know right. Like this guy I was dating one time. He told me he was a broker for a small law firm."

"A law firm?"

"Umm huh, so I asked him question after question. He couldn't tell me the name of the law firm. What he did as a broker for the law firm? Each lie just let me know he was broker and broker."

Marla laughed, "Gia, you're crazy."

"I'm just saying. If you're unemployed, don't lie about it. I know if I was unemployed and somebody asked me about it. I would be like 'Yeah, I'm just sitting on my ass. What you got to say about that, huh? You gon' pay my bills?' Uh, these people know not to mess with me. But Melanie, she has to make it seem like she's doing better than everyone else…. Thinking she is all high and mighty placing her own damn self on a pedestal…Living solely off her inheritance. Wish I was so lucky… Yeah, somebody definitely needs to knock her off that damn high horse."

Marla closed her eyes again. "If she keeps messing with me, I just might be the one."

CHAPTER 16

As Laila sat at the bar, she stared at the clock. A group of people, laughing and talking, were preparing to leave, but she shared none of their emotions. She began to drink her sorrows away. The cold air that matched the coldness in her heart brushed her neck as the door closed behind the happy crowd. She could feel the fine hairs on the back of her neck stand. She rubbed her neck, and someone placed his hand on her shoulder. She jumped and quickly looked up; it was Alonzo.

"Hi," he sat beside her on the vacant bar stool.

"Hi," she sipped her drink.

"I knew I would find you here."

"And here I am."

"I've seen your car parked here on several occasions. Are you okay?"

"Yes, everything is perfect," she took a huge swig.

He shook his head, "Hmm … perfect, eh?"

Just as she was about to take another sip, he took the glass out of her hand, his hand gently brushing hers. She glared at him. He had some nerve.

"We'll have two bottles of water," he told the bartender, holding up two fingers. He looked at Laila, "So after all of this time you're still feeling my boy."

Sounding like a teenage girl, "What? I don't like that boy."

"That's not what it looks like at the wedding rehearsals. It seems like, to me, it's killing you to be there."

The bartender handed him the bottles of Dasani water.

"No, it's not. I'm happy to see my friends getting married," she zoned out and looked like she was in a daze, "over and over and over again."

"You know I know you, right? I know when you're happy, mad, sad, and I especially know when you don't want to be bothered."

"Well, you're not getting the message right now," she rolled her eyes. He smiled as he skillfully twisted the top off each bottle as if he wanted to show the world he was a pro at any task- big or small. He grabbed two red napkins and used them as coasters.

"I know we didn't talk that much in high school," Alonzo sipped his water.

"No, we didn't. *You* were too busy trying to get in my pants to hold a normal conversation."

"Yeah, I had game back then," he said.

She rolled her eyes again. "That's what you called it? Game? Humph…"

"Yep, that's exactly what I had. I got everyone I really wanted…except you."

She quickly looked at him, then smirked, "Oh, give me a break."

"It's true, but you had your eyes fixated on Quinton though," he slid his bar stool closer to her. She raised her brows at him. "Laila, why can't you let the man go?"

She didn't bother to respond.

"Don't tell me you're in love with him. You haven't seen each other in damn near eight years."

Her heart began to ache. She felt like a ton of bricks were around her heart and it was pounding harder with each breath, trying to break free.

SHE'S MARRYING MY MAN

She let out a deep sigh. "I know, I know," she turned to him, "but have you ever wanted something so bad that you hope someday you'll get it?

He swallowed, "Yes."

"And once you realize you can't ever obtain it, it hurts like hell," she sipped her water.

"Yeah it does," he studied her face, "I know you're hurting, Laila."

"I am," she admitted.

"And I'm not trying to come on to you when I say this," he held up his hands, "but I'll help you get through this. Okay? Just let my boy be happy. He won't be … *unless* he knows you've moved on …You don't want to ruin your friendship with Melanie, do you?"

Laila shook her head, and then pouted, "But I had him first."

He gave her a half-smile and then licked his lips, "Well, if he wanted you and I mean *really* wanted you, he would have found you and he sure as hell wouldn't have hooked up with your girlfriend."

Laila couldn't deny it; he made a valid point. She sighed, "Yeah, that's true."

He got up and offered his hand to her. "So can I help you get through this? Will you let me take you home?"

She gulped the rest of her water. "Yeah, I guess," she accepted his hand, and he helped her to her feet. He escorted her out of the bar with her arm wrapped around his neck.

CHAPTER 17

Laila had been feeling upset and sick from what she had done with Quinton. It took all of the strength in her body to stomach seeing Quinton and Melanie together. She wanted to get her mind off them. She wanted to get away from them.

Alonzo had asked to take her out when he drove her home from the bar. Laila reluctantly agreed and he promptly showed up the next night at 7 and took her to a restaurant in Atlanta.

"So, people actually trust you with their portfolios?"

"Oh, yes, you'll be surprised at how quick rich white women are to receive my services."

Laila smirked, "Umm, huh." She knew he was referring to his different sex escapades.

"Naw, to be real, most of my clientele are upper-middle class African Americans. Can you believe that? A lot of us have a substantial amount of money in the South."

"Bet it's not liquid," Laila said dryly.

He shook his head, "If you'd like, I can help plan your future," he gave her his card, "but I only speak business in my office," he bit his bottom lip.

"Okay,"

"Yep, I got the best marketer in the game. Because of Q, I pull more clients than anyone at my firm."

"Well, that's good for you."

"So Laila McKee is the Director of Diversity Relations."

Laila rolled her eyes. "Come on with the nasty, corny line."

He started laughing.

"Your corny line, Alonzo. I know you."

"What did you think I was going to say?"

"Something like, 'Well, I'm diverse and I love relations.'"

"Aw hell naw," he burst out laughing.

"So you weren't going to say that?"

He wouldn't stop laughing, he turned red.

"Naw... I can't lie. I was thinking that, but I wasn't going to say anything."

"Aw ha...I knew it,"

"Girl, you know me too well."

"No, you dropped your silly lines too many times."

He finally calmed down, "I never would have thought you'd be working at a bank, I thought you'd be a writer."

"Really?"

"Yea, I remember in high school, you would always be writing in a journal. You would get pissed if anybody tried to touch it."

"Yeah, and you were the main one who tried to take it from me."

"And I still cringe whenever a woman's knee comes too close to my lower region."

"Sorry about that."

"You still keep a journal?"

"Yes, on my nightstand, but I only write in it when something is troubling me."

"Okay, well, I guess that is good therapy... Letting your feelings out,"

"Yes, I have to let them out in some way."

"Personally, I'll just cuss out anyone that pisses me off."

"That's the difference between you and me. I'm not confrontational."

"Says the lady who kicked my balls."

"Hey, I already apologized," she said, then discussed the aforementioned. "I just don't like drama."

"I understand that, but being passive allows for people to walk over you."

"What do you mean by that?" he was sending her a hint that she received loud and clear. She was just offended by it. What gave him the audacity to discuss her friendship with Melanie?

"Oh, nothing. I just… never mind," he looked away. "Waitress, can I get another refill on the tea?"

"Me too, and can you bring me a small bowl of lemon wedges."

The waitress nodded. Alonzo stared at Laila.

"What?"

"Nothing. I'm just surprised you agreed to go on a date with me."

"Well, I have nothing else better to do. It beats being forced to do something with Melanie or watch her fawn all over Quinton."

"Likewise," Alonzo said, "I think they're a little over the top with all of the 'lovey dovey' bullshit."

"She stepped onto my lanai and-"

"Oh, you have a lanai," he looked intrigued. Laila smiled; he was the first person who didn't blast her for using that term instead of patio. "Maybe we can sit around and have drinks out there sometimes. *Nonalcoholic* drinks."

"Ha ha …very funny," she shook her head, licked her lips, and coyly said, "We'll see."

The waitress approached them with a pitcher of tea and the bowl of lemon wedges. She placed the bowl on the table and refilled the glasses. Alonzo stared at Laila as she placed three lemons in her glass of tea. "So you and

Quinton?"

She sighed. "I figured you were the one he called on." At first, she wasn't sure if he knew. She knew Quinton and Alonzo told each other everything and helped each other out of jams, but since she had been talking to Alonzo, he had never made any indication that he knew her and Quinton had sex until now.

"Yeah, I can't believe you actually had it in you to do it."

She sipped her drink. "Me either."

"You must have been pretty angry to get Melanie back like that."

"I don't know. I just wasn't thinking."

"But why go about it that way?"

"What do you mean?"

"Why accept to be Melanie's maid of honor? Why didn't you just cuss her out…kick her ass…something?"

"I asked myself those exact questions. I just wanted to be the bigger person, you know, rise above it all. I just didn't know I still had deep feelings for Quinton. He just showed up at my door, looking and smelling so good. I had been drinking and plus I hadn't had se-" she paused.

"Say what? You haven't had what?"

"That's more of a personal matter that I'd rather not discuss."

"Aw come on. It's me, Alonzo. You can talk to me. So you were celibate for a while?"

She sighed, "Yes, I was for almost a year and a half."

"Really?" he leaned forward, "you wanna know a secret?"

Laila smirked and waited for his big reveal.

"I'm celibate now."

Laila shook her head, "What? You are lying."

"No, I'm for real. It's been just six months for me, but I'm abstaining."

"Until when? Tomorrow?"

"I don't know. I'm just tired of the same type of

woman. You know what I mean?"

"All too well."

"I mean most of them are beautiful. Some have one or two children. Some don't, but they are always after money and jump from man to man to get more."

"Well, you jump from woman to woman."

"I did. I *jumped* from one woman to the other because I wanted complete satisfaction. One woman would fulfill a desire that another couldn't. I craved… hell, I was on a quest to find that perfect woman who knew exactly how to please me, but I never found her. Then, I finally realized I may not ever find her. That's when I stopped; I wanted to reassess my life. Now, I know that I want a nice faithful hard-working woman who I can love physically and emotionally."

"You want the heart, body, mind, and soul. Yea, yea," Laila said, "Good luck with that."

"It's just hard to find a good woman. Either she is too focused on her career or she lets the man become her entire life. I prefer career-oriented women. Lately, I've been talking to successful women who know how to balance their professional and personal lives…women who would have sex before looking at any law documents, police files, or ungraded papers."

"Wait a minute. You dated a police officer."

"Oh yes. Those handcuffs came in handy. That woman was kinky, but she was crazy as hell. One night she spotted another female in the car with me, so she pulled me over, busted my taillight with her nightstick, and wrote me a ticket for a broken taillight."

"Really?"

"Yeah, she called me and apologized. She told me she tore the ticket, then she broke up with me. She told me her partner finally admitted he had feelings for her and I was happy as hell not to have a lady of the law stalking me."

"Wow."

"I've set high standards for myself now though."

"High standards?"

"Yes, she has to have the whole package. She has to be up there with you."

"With me? What do you mean by that?"

"She has to be kind, beautiful, intelligent, and her smile has to light up the entire room. She has to know what she wants in life and fights until it's finally hers."

When he said that she thought of Quinton, *Am I supposed to fight for him?*

He went on. "She isn't promiscuous. She goes out of her way to help anyone she can. She tries to avoid drama and confrontation. When she falls in love with me, her eyes are staying on me and only me, and that is you."

Laila shook her head. *Same Alonzo. He still doesn't know what he's talking about.*

"Well, I'm nothing like the woman you just described."

"Laila, we're all human. So you made a mistake… don't beat yourself up over that."

"But what if it wasn't a mistake?"

"Well, it's your life. It's whatever you think."

She sighed, "I became celibate because I got tired of sleeping with the same boring uptight wall street journal reading, penny loafer wearing blowhards."

He shook his head and chuckled.

She continued, "They were doctors, surgeons, and lawyers who were simply corny and boring. Many of whom were republicans, so the only thing that heated them up was politics."

"Republicans? So you dated white men?"

"Nope. You know there are many black people who are Republicans, Tom Joiner and . . . I think Melanie is even a Republican."

"Hmm, remind me to have a talk with her," he said, "but answer my question, have you dated outside of your race?"

"I've dated a Caucasian and an Asian. The la-"

"I love me some Asian women … umm, I think this

celibacy thing is getting to me. Damn, I need some… Hey, aren't you mixed with Asian?"

"My grandma was, but as I was saying, my last boyfriend didn't want to go out or do anything. He didn't even want to sit home and watch movies. His idea of a good time was going to Borders so he could buy the latest John Grisham book or Jason Bourne novel, and recording the State of the Union Address, so he could watch it over and over again."

"So how was the sex?"

"Boring."

"I bet you he came in probably five minutes."

"Uh, if that."

"So how many men have you slept with?"

"Uh, that's personal."

"Well, we're friends aren't we?" he grinned, and then sounded like a kid, "I'll tell you mine if you tell me yours."

"Well, a woman never reveals her number. Ever."

"Hmm…I bet I can count on one hand."

"Umm huh," Laila nodded.

"I know it's at least two but no more than five."

Laila smiled. He was close.

"What about you?"

"Twenty-five."

"Twenty-five?"

"Yes, exactly twenty-five."

"Well, that's less than I thought," Laila said. *He knows he's lying, I can name twenty-five girls he slept with in high school. But hey, what do I care?*

"Yeah, most of those women, I'd break up with them, then I would get a new girlfriend. Then, I would cheat on my new girlfriend with some of my exes."

"Any one night stands?"

"Of course, but it wasn't that many. You ever had a one night stand?"

"I don't know," she said sarcastically, "Let's see, what have I done lately?"

"Aw, you know him and you two have history."

"Yeah,"

"You never know he might come knocking on your door tonight for round two."

"Well, I won't be home."

"So you're willing to be out with me until the wee hours of the morning?"

"Sure why not? The latest I've ever been out was 2 a.m."

"You must have been at some club spot."

"Yeah, but that was in my early 20's."

"Don't you know fun is where you make it? You don't have to be clubbin' to have fun."

"Really? So what can we possibly do until the wee hours of the morning?"

"Oh, I can think of a few things," he had a devious look on his face.

"Ugh, you're nasty," she shook her head, "I just left myself wide open for that one."

"Yes," he licked his lips, "Wide open."

Laila felt slightly uncomfortable with the way he was looking at her, but it had been a while since a man gave her this much attention. Not even Quinton had talked to her this much.

CHAPTER 18

"Alonzo and I have been hanging out lately."

"For real?" Gia was styling her hair in Laila's guestroom.

"Yes, we have," she stared at her reflection in the mirror as she sat in a chair in front of the chest of drawers.

"Okay, so you got revenge on the bitch, now you're gettin' revenge on Quinton."

Laila shook her head, "It's-"

"Alright. I have a new level of respect for you. I'ma have to induct you into the bad girls' club."

"Gia, it's nothing like that. Alonzo is just," Laila thought for a moment, "helping me get over Quinton."

Gia raised her brow and looked in the mirror at her. "And whose *helping* do you like best? Alonzo or Quinton's?"

"Hey," Laila swung her arm back and hit Gia's leg. Gia started laughing. "Alonzo and I haven't had sex, and we're not going to."

"Come on girl. You've dipped into the pot, you might as well stick your whole spoon in."

"What?" Laila wrinkled her brows, "what in the world are you talking about?"

"I don't know. I heard Big Ma say it the other day or something of that affect. What I'm saying is you took your chance with Quinton, you might as well go all the way with Alonzo."

"No, no… there is absolutely no way."

"Girl, you need to stop playing and get with that. Who knows…you two might actually form a real relationship."

"Alonzo and I? In a real relationship?" they burst out laughing.

"Yeah, that ain't Alonzo at all. I will shake the hand of the woman who gets him to settle down."

CHAPTER 19

Kecia was at home getting ready to go hang out with Laila and Gia. She walked across her bedroom, sprayed on her perfume, grabbed her purse and made her way down the hall. She heard the television in the living room and didn't remember turning it on. With her car keys rattling in her hand, she looked on the dining table for her remote.

"And where do you think you're going?" she heard Leonard ask. She rolled her eyes and turned to see him sitting on her couch.

"Out," she responded dryly.

He got up, leaned against the arm of her sofa and folded his arms. "And do pretell where that might be."
She smirked, "None of your business."

He looked at her from head to toe; she was dressed in denim skinny jeans, a white tank top, with a draped purple cardigan.

"If it's concerning you, then it *is* my business," he said with a smug look on his face, "You know...you've been acting strange since your little friend came back to town."

"Oh, *I've* been acting strange?" she asked in disbelief with her hand resting on her chest.

"Yes, you've been gone almost every night this week …going to rehearsal?" he paced around, "How dumb are they that they can't figure out how to walk down a damn aisle."

Kecia clenched her jaws to hold back the words she wanted to spurt out.

He continued, "When is the next rehearsal?"

"I don't know," she quickly said with an attitude.

"Well, let me know so I can sit in and see what's going on."

She smirked, "You can't. It's a closed rehearsal. Melanie only wants the wedding party to attend."

"They may not be having that many rehearsals. That may just be your excuse."

"My excuse?" she asked, "Ta, what's your excuse for being over here at my apartment every evening? Before now, I would beg your ass to come over. I would wait for you and sometimes you wouldn't even show up. So why now? Huh?"

He didn't respond. He just looked at her.

She went on, "Now that I have something to do. You wanna be here all up under my ass."

"Hmm, why are you getting defensive? You're jumping down my throat using all of that foul language…Oh, I think you're hiding something. You're sneaking around on me, aren't you?"

Kecia couldn't believe what she was hearing, "What?"

"Answer the question, Kecia!"

"No! Okay?" she glanced at her dining room table, "But I sho'll as hell wish I was."

"What did you just say?"

She shook her head and looked at him, "I just don't get you, Leonard. We don't go out anymore. I have to beg you to come to get-togethers … We don't go on trips-"

"I told you-"

"The damn quota…I know," she said, "You don't make any romantic gestures. You don't do a damn thing but give me hell."

"I would do more and give you more if you'd just do the things I ask you to do."

"Like what? Lose weight?" she folded her arms, "Well, if I was cheating, then *bae-bae* that man would be enjoying all of dis right here, wouldn't he? With no complaints."

"Sex is sex, Kecia. Size doesn't matter behind closed doors."

"Keep thinkin' that," she smirked.

"So is that it? Have I pushed you into the arms of someone else?"

"If that was the case, I would have been don' dropped yo' corny little ass. Now, if you'll excuse me," she walked towards the door.

"We're not finished talking."

"Oh yes we are," she said, "I'm finna go and I ain't gotta run shit by you cuz one, I'm grown, two, this is my place and I pay *all* the bills up in here, and three, my birth certificate clearly states that my daddy is Kenneth Jinard Jones."

She opened the door and looked back at Leonard. "And F-Y-I…I do more for you than anyone ever will. So you can either step up and be my man or get the fuck out of my life," then slammed the door behind her.

CHAPTER 20

It was laundry day and Kecia showed up at Laila's home bright and early. She knew Kecia had something on her mind. She beat around the bush asking Laila random questions and following her around as she gathered her clothes and walked to the wash room. Once Laila was finished, she brought her clothes into the living room and the two began folding clothes in silence.

"Laila," she finally said, "I've been proud of you for most of your life. No matter what lemons life has always thrown you. You've always seem to keep a smile and serve up some lemonade or sweet tea drenched in lemons."

Laila shook her head as she started folding her robes.

"I mean, you went to college and even though we both talked about it, you went ahead and got your Master's. You have an excellent career and a beautiful home. You do well in every aspect of your life except your love life."

"Kecia, no offense, but my love life is none of your concern."

"You're my friend, aren't you? You've told me what you think of Leonard because you've dated guys like him."

Laila sighed, "Yeah until you shu-"

"Do you want to know why everything in your life is

going great but your love life?"

Laila smirked, "Why Kecia?"

"Because you're stuck in the past," she looked at her, "No one can be successful when they're stuck in the past. What good can you possibly do in the future, if you're constantly stuck in the past? What new things can you achieve? What new relationships will fester? If you're still dwelling on what could have been…you can't change the past nor can you go back. I've seen you move on from so many things but you just can't seem to shake Quinton. Personally, I don't see what's so amazing about him. But hey, everyone has their own taste."

"Kecia."

"Laila, please move on from Quinton because if you don't you might just ruin the good things you have going on in your life."

"Why do you constantly think I'm holding things in and holding on to Quinton? I'm not and I'm doing just fine."

"No you're not. Laila, I keep telling you that it's not healthy. You're going to keep being nice and holding all of that anger and pain in until one day you will explode."

"Kecia,"

"It's been years. You have years of pinned up negative feelings and frustration against your parents, kids in high school, old co-workers, ex-boyfriends, old friends, the people in this town, Quinton, and Melanie. You can't just hold that in, you have to talk about it. If not to Gia or me, get a counselor."

"Kecia, I'm not crazy. I don't need professional help."

"I didn't say you were, honey, but you have to clear your mind. You don't have to be crazy to have the urge to maintain your sanity. Laila, once you get all of that out of your mind, you will see things more clearly. You will stop worrying about Quinton; you will tell Melanie where she can go, and darling, you will find inner peace, and the man of your dreams will find you."

Laila sighed and looked at her, "You're right Kecia. I hear what you're saying, so will *you* finally listen to me and Gia now?"

"Oh not this again,"

"You see, Kecia," Laila said, "You snap and shut Gia and I out each time we mention Leonard now."

Kecia exhaled, "Okay, I'll listen to you, Laila."

"I've always admired your confidence and I love the way you tell it like it is and voice your opinion without caring what the reaction may be. You are not shy and go after whatever you want…"

"But," Kecia said.

"But, when it comes to men, you settle like you think you're not good enough to have a good man. Over the years, you've been with unattractive men with equally unattractive attitudes. They've demeaned you, taken from you, and treated you like you're nothing. You've dated quite a few handsome, nice men, but Kecia they were too boring or lame for you, so you let them go. Then, you met Leonard, the 'finest' of them all, and it's like you thought you hit the jackpot. You didn't, he did. And now, he's treating you worse than any of those men combined. You don't deserve to be insulted and controlled like this."

"Okay, let's get one thing straight, he doesn't control me," Kecia snapped.

"He may not control every aspect of your life, but he's trying to run your food intake with an iron fist,"

"Yeah, he has been getting out of hand with that."

"You're beautiful, Kecia, the way you are. He has no right to change you whether he's your boyfriend or husband. You lose weight only if you want to. No one should be forced to lose weight." Laila sighed, "And the last time I checked, the doctor gave you a clean bill of health."

"Yeah, he did."

"Now, you bit my head off when I mentioned his quote-unquote cousin, but I'll just say be watchful."

"I will," she said, "Leonard and I are happy and we have a solid monogamous relationship. It's just our season to face some drama. We'll come out on top," she said in an unenthusiastic tone.

"I know you will, Kecia," Laila said, and then repeated in almost a whisper, "I know you will."

CHAPTER 21

After her conversation with Kecia, Laila was ready to get her mind off Quinton. She didn't want to even think about Kecia's problems with Leonard. She walked into her kitchen and started preparing for her evening with Alonzo. She was excited. It was her first time cooking a meal for a man at her new home. He promptly showed up at seven and quickly devoured the food.

"Umm, I loved dinner and *you* actually cooked each dish?"

"Yes, I can cook."

"Oh cuz I remember in Home Ec, you burnt the hell out of that turkey,"

"Aw shut up," she said, "I remember a certain someone always coming to my station to bother me and taste my goodies."

"Yea, and I didn't miss a Wednesday."

She smiled.

"I hope you left some room for dessert."

"Dessert? Dang, what did I do to deserve all of this,"

She sat a slice of pie in front of him.

"Strawberry cheesecake. That's my favorite dessert.

How did you know?"

"I see you don't remember everything," she smiled, "In high school, every single time they served strawberry cheesecake, you would go up and down the rows of the cafeteria collecting slices. You would always beat Taaz and the other guys to us, so you could have all four slices to yourself. We would watch you go back to your seat, line the slices and make a full pie."

He laughed.

"We would watch you gobble all that down before Mrs. Sims would tell us it's time to go."

"Yeah, those cartons of milk I drank to wash it all down had me racing to the bathroom all fourth period."

"I was amazed at how it didn't make you sick. Thank goodness they only served it twice a month."

"Yeah,"

"You wanna know a secret?"

"What?"

She came across the table. "Strawberry cheesecake had always been my favorite dessert too." Alonzo smiled, realizing that she had made such a kind gesture in high school.

"Come on,"

"Where are we going? To your lanai?"

"Yea, you said you wanted to look at the stars."

They sat in her lounge chairs.

"Damn, it feels good out here."

"It does, doesn't it?" she smiled, gazing up at the sky and breathing in the cool fresh air.

"Whoa, you have this nice backyard and you're not doing anything with it."

"Well, what do you think I should do with it?"

"Get a good landscaper or maybe a pool."

"A pool? No, there is no way my children will live in a home with a pool in the backyard. They could easily slip away from me and…no, it's too dangerous."

"Aw, so you are planning on having kids in the future,

so does that mean marriage is still in the cards?"

"Yes, it is. I will find the perfect man someday and we'll get married and have a family."

"Well, you know the bible says when a *man* findeth a woman, *he* findeth a good thing."

"Yes, I've heard that a time or two," Laila said stubbornly, "Well, either way, we'll meet."

He shook his head, "Okay."

"So how about you? Is marriage in the cards for you?"

"Of course."

Laila laughed.

"Hey, why does everyone find that funny?"

"You can't be serious. The king of all ladies' men tied down to one woman? Please."

"Hey, I'm not trying to become some 60-year-old player popping pills trying to hit a woman in every age group. I want a wife to have children with and grow old with her and satisfy her every need for the rest of our lives."

"Aww. Well, I guess it's okay for you to dream."

"Wow, you're supposed to be my girl, you know my dawg or whatever… where's the faith at?"

"Ta, my faith left with my parents."

"Wha-"

"So how do you plan on finding your wife?" She veered him back to the subject they were on.

"I don't know. When I meet her, I'll just know. Every bone in my body will yearn for her. My heart will ache for her to be next to me each day I wake up."

"Whoa, that almost sounded romantic, then I realized who was speaking those words," Laila shook her head.

"Dang, you're something else, girl."

Laila looked away.

"So, um…you never really told me why your parents left."

"I haven't really told anybody not even Gia and Kecia,"

"Whoa, it's that major?"

"Yeah," she sighed, "You know my boss, the owner of my bank. Well, he and my mom have known each other for years since I was a little girl. She had been cheating on my father with him on and off since she first started working at his old bank."

"Hold on…with that short, fat white man?"

"Well, no he didn't always look like that," then in a British accent, "He was actually quite smashing."

"What? Where that come from?"

"I don't know," she laughed, "It took me a while, but I finally put two and two together when I was a teen. I was just too scared to confront her. Then, when I was in college, I came home and I caught him coming out of my parents' bedroom, zipping up his pants. My mother and I had gotten into a heated argument. I told her it was not fair to Dad for her to do that to him and she had been forcing me to live with the secret. Little did I know, my dad had come home early to surprise my mom for their anniversary, and he overheard us arguing."

"He used to drive trucks, didn't he?"

She nodded.

"So what did he do?"

"He slowly walked into the room, put down his gift and walked out. We tried to talk to him, but he wanted nothing to do with us…with me. He hopped in his truck and finally spoke to my mother. He told her that he wanted a divorce and sped off…and that was the last time I saw him. My mother slapped me as hard as she could and told me to get out of her house and never come back. I went back to school and the next thing I knew, she had shipped the things I valued most to my university address. I went home and there was a for sale sign in the yard. I tried to use my key, but I couldn't get in. I looked in the bare windows and there was nothing left. Nothing…"

"Damn, I can't believe they did that to you."

She nodded, "No one would tell me anything. It's like my parents went their separate ways and my entire life…my family…my past disappeared without a trace."

He got up, sat right next to her on her lounge chair, and held her.

"My graduation came and no sign of my parents. No sign… Now, people are more willing to talk about them. I've heard my father lives overseas probably in Asia, with a whole new life and family."

"I can definitely relate to that."

"And I heard my mother lives up north with her baby sister. I've sent my aunt countless letters and made countless phone calls. She would never write back and never pick up the phone. Soon, numbers became disconnected and letters were returned. So, here I am, with Kecia, Gia, and sometimes, Melanie," she smiled, "And I'm still dreaming of the perfect husband and my very own family."

"That's deep, Laila. I never knew you went through all of that."

"When I moved back into town, my mother's lover wouldn't give me a job at first. He told me there were no open positions though I clearly saw three spots were available online… loan officer, bank teller, and secretary. I just looked at him. As I was about to storm out of the bank, his wife walked in and greeted me. His face turned red and he rushed over to us. And, the next thing I knew he had created a position just for me and tacked on the loan officer duties. I guess to keep my mouth shut. My mother had always used manipulation and blackmail with him countless times, so I guess he was afraid I would do the same."

"Wow, your mother was a *bad* woman, huh?"

"Yes, but as I look back, I'm starting to wonder, am I truly my mother's child? Since I can remember, I've always longed for another woman's man. I wanted Quinton and the whole time he belonged to someone else and then I sleep with him, knowing he belongs to Melanie now. Am I just like her?"

"Laila, Laila," he was still holding her, "No, you're nothing like your mother. You're beautiful, honest, loyal, and human—we all make mistakes. It is up to us to learn from them and never repeat those mistakes. Okay?" he squeezed her, "You hear me?"

She nodded. She was surprised that she finally opened up to someone and it was Alonzo of all people. It felt as if a heavy load was slowly lifted from her.

"You will have that family and your life won't mirror your parents' lives. You're better than that, Laila. I believe it."

She took a deep breath.

"The question is do you believe it?"

"I do," she finally managed to say. Alonzo blew his breath.

"Now, come on. Let's talk about transforming this yard into a magical place for your family with shallow koi ponds, stone walkways, exotic flowers, stringed lights, and beautiful arcs."

Laila smiled as he pulled her to her feet.

***

Kecia and Gia were caught in a predicament they did not want to be in-- hanging out with Melanie at Gia's apartment.

Melanie just looked at them as Kecia was surfing the web on her phone and Gia was filing her fingernails.

"So, where's Laila?"

"Out with her lil' friend somewhere," Gia said in between blowing her nails.

"Oh, those two have really been at it,"

"Um huh," Kecia said, "So um…I have a question. When did you and Quinton get engaged?"

"In January,"

"January, dang you sho'll in a rush to marry him,"

"Um huh," Kecia looked at her stomach, "you sure you're not-"

"Don't be ridiculous," Melanie laughed it off, "You

know I am above having a *shotgun* wedding."

"Just because you get married with a baby in yo' belly don't make you lower than anybody."

"Thank you,"

Melanie rolled her eyes.

"So you two chose April 22nd together?"

"Yes, well no…I wanted us to get married on the 2nd, but Quinton wanted to make sure Taaz would be here since he's an offshore driller. He works two weeks consecutively, and he returns home for two we-"

"Yeah, yeah, we know how it works, Melanie."

"You know my brothers, Ronnie and Gavin work off sho'."

"So you have everything all set for the wedding?" Kecia asked.

"Just about. I've already ordered the extravagant décor since Quinton was against hiring a wedding planner. I've had to depend on Aunt Judy to pull this together."

"Umm…Huh,"

"But Quinton insisted on borrowing items from family members and buying cheap decorations for the reception at the low-end retailers such as Wal-Mart and the general stores."

Kecia raised her brows.

"You mean Dollar General and Family Dollar," Gia corrected her.

"So I take it that Quinton designed the invitations and the wedding programs?"

"Yeah, and we haven't laid our eyes on not one of yo' invitations."

Melanie sighed, "Well, verbal invitations always trump a piece of stationary when it comes to the people who are near and dear to your heart, don't you think?"

Gia smirked.

"And to answer your question, Kecia … No, Quinton wanted to design them, but I thought it was best to order some eloquent ones that I stumbled upon online."

"Wow, ain't that what he do for a living?"

"Not anymore. He was a Graphic Designer, but now he's an-"

"Damn, Melanie. You're insulting the man's livelihood."

"Umm huh…you're telling him, 'you can't do *ish* for me, you can't even design my damn wedding programs.' Where the *we* at, Melanie?"

"Gia does make a valid point, Melanie. Are you allowing Quinton to have *any* say?"

"Oh come on, girls. He's a man. You know they don't like to be bogged down with pla-"

"Blah, blah, blah, Melanie," Gia cut her off.

"Well, since I've known Quinton he's been designing flyers and brochures for community dances, parties, school events…he even created our damn graduation program," Kecia said.

"He sho'll did, so how in the hmmm…" Gia buzzed, "He don't wanna be *bogged* down with stuff for *his* wedding."

They both stared at Melanie, waiting for her answer.

"You see? This is exactly why I don't like to be alone with you two," she began gathering her things, "You always gang up on me. It's been this way since high school."

She stood, eyed them, and took a deep breath.

"You ladies are either for me or against me. And, if you're against me, then stay the hell away from my wedding."

She walked towards the door.

"Uh, somebody don' grew some balls."

"Melanie," Kecia called as the door slammed.

"Girl, let that bitch go," she said, "Somebody gon' back out of helping her do something and she gon' come right back, kissing our asses, so *we* can get it done."

"You know what? You're right. I think the only reason she asked us to be in the wedding is because none of her snobby lil' friends would come down here and she needed enough bridesmaids to balance out Quinton's side."

"I know that's what it is."

CHAPTER 22

Alonzo surprised Laila at her home and invited her to go with him to the spring parade on the court square. They were in his silver Mercedes. He quickly got out and opened her door. She could hear the faint sound of a band in the distance. It was a beautiful night; the full moon illuminated the sky and the stars sparkled brightly. A huge crowd was around the town square, so they walked down the sidewalk away from the ruckus.

There were tables set up along the sidewalk. People were selling nachos, flowers, funnel cakes, lemonade, and other items. They met a few people as they walked and talked. Laila laughed at one of Alonzo's many jokes. It was refreshing for her to actually laugh and enjoy herself for a change. He slyly placed his hand in hers. She looked down, but didn't pull her hand away. It was a big step for her because in high school, she would have jerked away and slapped him. Laila noticed the white cloth-covered tables displayed delectable food, then one table caught her eye.

"Ooo, chocolate covered strawberries."

A white woman with strawberry blonde hair smiled at them.

"Hi, how are you doing this evening?"

"We're fine."

"Would like to buy some strawberries?"

"Yes, we would like a dozen and a single."

He handed money to her, and she gave him a white box and a strawberry wrapped in wax paper. He turned to Laila.

"Sweets for the lady."

He fed her the strawberry. The creamy chocolate texture and strawberry juice bursting in her mouth made a warm feeling come over her body. She closed her eyes as she indulged in her two favorite things combined as one. She opened her eyes and Alonzo was staring at her intensely with a sexy look on his face. A strange feeling came over her that felt like a tingling sensation. Laila heard someone clear his throat. They both looked around; Melanie and Quinton were standing on the sidewalk gazing at them. They both jumped in surprise and Alonzo quickly threw the remainder of the strawberry in a trash can by the table.

"Oh, hey y'all," Alonzo said while scratching the back of head. The two looked guilty.

Melanie smiled, "Uh huh. We caught you."

Laila smiled awkwardly, "Yeah, you caught us."

Quinton asked, "So how long has this been going on?"

Laila looked at him. Her heart skipped a beat. She wished she was walking around with Quinton and sharing fruit with him. Yet, there he was standing in front of her, holding hands with Melanie and looking at her with menacing eyes like she was cheating on him. "Um, not too long."

Melanie chimed in. "So are you two together?"

"I wouldn't say together, but we-"

"We-We've been dating for a little while now," Alonzo answered for her.

Melanie smiled at her, "So Alonzo is the one you've been getting wild with all along. That explains the Curve."

Looking at Quinton, Alonzo smiled, "Yeah, I'm the

one."

Melanie held Quinton's arm and looked at him, "Baby, they've been keeping a secret from us." She gasped, "And that also explains why you were so upset when I was trying to fix you up at the engagement party."

Laila gave a fake bashful smile.

Alonzo came up with another lie. "We were going to come clean, but we wanted all of the attention to be on you two since your wedding is coming up."

"Aw, isn't that sweet, honey," Melanie said to Quinton.

"Yeah, sweet," he said through gritted teeth. "So y'all got together before or after we came to town?"

"After," Laila said.

"Before," he said, "Don't be modest honey," he wrapped his arm around Laila and squeezed her, then looked at Quinton and Melanie, "About three weeks ago, I saw Laila in the parking lot at her bank. I was passing through and when I saw her, I just had to pull in and speak, so that's how we met up again …Things just kind of happened from there."

Well, I have to give it to him. That's a good lie especially since that's how Quinton and Melanie saw me the other day. I wonder if Quinton had already told Alonzo about that awkward encounter.

"Oh really?" Quinton asked as if he had discovered the real truth behind Laila and Alonzo.

"Well, you two kept that secret from us very well."

"Yea, just like you and Quinton did," Laila said. Alonzo raised his brows, surprised that she had made her smart comment.

"Touché," Melanie said.

Quinton was staring at Alonzo intensely yet Melanie didn't notice. She was too busy looking at the *new couple*.

"Laila, can I talk to you for a moment?"

"Sure," they walked down the sidewalk and stood a small distance from the guys.

"Way to go girl," then she had no further interest in Laila and Alonzo. She started talking about her wedding plans once again.

Typical. No matter what happens, it's all about Melanie.

Meanwhile, the guys were having a private conversation of their own.

Quinton bit his lip and looked at Alonzo, "So you and Laila?"

"Yeah, you're not mad. Are you?"

"Naw man," he glanced over at the ladies and then looked Alonzo straight in the eye, "So are you sleeping with her?"

"For your sake, I am… unless you want Melanie to know who was really over her best friend's house."

Quinton raised his eyebrows at him and didn't respond.

"Relax man. I had to lie about me and her meeting up to throw your girl off. I'm just looking out for you."

Quinton looked at him in disbelief.

"I'm taking Laila off your hands, so you can be with Melanie without any distractions." Melanie and Laila rejoined the guys.

"You ready, baby?" Melanie asked Quinton, but Quinton was still staring at Alonzo.

Alonzo patted Quinton on his shoulder. "One day, you'll be thanking me for being your best man."

Melanie said, "Hey, maybe one day this week we can go on a double date."

Laila tried to think of the perfect excuse, "Uhh no, I-"

Alonzo interrupted, "You know what that's a good ass idea. Isn't it Quinton?"

What?

"Yes, I think we need some time to chill together." Quinton said.

Melanie smiled once again. "Well, how does Tuesday night sound?"

"Perfect," Alonzo said.

"Well, it's a date."

"I guess it is," Laila finally said.

"Well, it's about that time for us to be getting back to

my hotel room. But first, we're going to drop by the store and get *us* some strawberries," she winked her eye at Laila and waved as they walked away.

"Save some for the honeymoon," Alonzo called.

"We will!" Melanie said.

CHAPTER 23

Kecia drove sixty-three miles to Atlanta for dinner. She'd had a long day, working her free period because the 5th grade teacher, Mrs. Beckford went into labor. Then, she was the monitor for the week and had to ensure that all of the 453 students made it safely on the bus all by herself since Ms. Sheila, the kindergarten teacher, had to leave early and Mr. Brown had to take an urgent phone call coincidentally as soon as the last bell rang. Once all of the kids were gone, Kecia had to join the other faculty members in the multi-purpose room for a mandatory teacher's meeting. Yet, they had to wait 20 minutes for the principal to arrive. Once he made his way to the meeting, it lasted for an hour and a half.

Kecia was pissed; she wanted to tell Mr. Brown a piece of her mind, but he would also be getting all of her pinned-up frustration that she had with Leonard and then, she would definitely be out of a job, so she kept her peace. After her long hectic day, she had to get away from it all – no cooking, no nosey, noisy neighbors, no self-absorbed friends, and thankfully, no Leonard.

She placed her black Altima on cruise control, turned her air on max, and leaned back as she felt the cold burst of air against her skin. She let out a calm sigh. While driving down the long stretch of highway, Kecia began to relax. Food, cold air, and driving had always made Kecia feel good no matter what was going on in her life.

Once she reached Atlanta, she couldn't find a place that she and Leonard had not been to during the early stages of their relationships, so she drove aimlessly around, then decided to go to the new barbeque restaurant that she hadn't visited yet.

Kecia was sitting alone at her table. Almost every table was filled, there was a lot of chatter and waitresses were bustling with drinks and food. The waitress placed her food on the table.

Taaz entered and looked around.

"Damn, it's crowded in here," he walked up to the front desk.

"Hey, do ya'll have a table for two available?"

"Uh, let's see," she looked around, "Aw yes. Follow me."

He was behind her at first, then people started to get up. He decided to go down a free aisle. Then, he saw Kecia. *Man, why she gotta be here?* He tried to dodge her, but he ran into more people getting up from their chairs. He was forced to walk down her aisle. He quickly passed without Kecia noticing him, then his phone rang.

"Hello?" he frowned, "What? You decided not to go out with me? Well, this is a fine damn time to tell me. What kind of … man whatever," he hung up and put his phone in his pocket. He turned around, then looked down at Kecia and saw her plate. He walked on, thought for a moment, then turned around and approached Kecia.

He looked at her plate and shook his head, "What you doing, man?"

She looked up and rolled her eyes. "Aw hell, I travel over 60 miles to have an evening to myself away from the people in Layville. And, here your ass is,"

"Well, I hope you don't think running into you

brightens my damn day."

"Well, get the hell on then."

"Man, whatever."

Kecia sighed, "Were you put on this earth to annoy me or something?"

"Maybe so, Ms. Bad Ass Attitude."

"Nosey Ass Negro,"

He bit his bottom lip and raised his brows, "You know you like it."

"Humph…"

"But for real though," he gestured at her plate, "what are you doing?"

"I'm sitting here minding my own business eating a salad and drinking a diet soda."

He sat down.

"Well, help yourself to a seat at *my* table," she said sarcastically.

He smirked, "What you're eating, you know that ain't you. Where's the ranch? The bacon? Cheese? Man, is that a lemon?" He attempted to touch the wedge on her plate, but she hit his hand.

"I am on a diet."

"A diet?" his eyes grew as big as Chris Tucker's. "This is not a diet, this is starvation. How you gon' get full off of that?"

"I'll manage," she looked at him, "What are you? Some health guru now?"

He ignored her question, "Who you doing this for? Him?"

"Myself. I have to be healthy, Taaz."

"Look at you, you are… you've always been healthy," he took a deep breath, "I know I've always talked about your weight ever since we were kids, but I don't be meaning no harm. I wouldn't want you to change…"

She looked down.

"… but he wants you to. Doesn't he? Don't lie."

She sighed, "Yes."

"Kecia,"

"Taaz, you don't get to tell me about my life. And you're not even a friend of mine. All *you* do is piss me off."

"Well, whether you like it or not, I've always been your friend, girl."

She smirked.

"Your annoying friend who loves pissing you off," he smiled, "but look, I'm not trying to do that right now so just listen to me."

She looked up at him.

"You don't need to be with somebody who isn't happy with the way you are."

"Well, ever since I've been dating, that's all they've ever worried about. 'When are you going to lose weight?' 'Damn girl, slow down you gone eat up the whole buffet.' Taaz, how do you think that makes me feel?"

"Well, you've been dating the wrong guys. You just haven't found the right one yet. Plenty of guys out there love a thick woman."

"You think so?"

"I know so. I don't care how the dude looks, how much he makes, or whatever. That doesn't give him an excuse to treat you like you're inferior."

"Inferior? Wow, somebody finally took my advice and got hooked on phonics." Kecia joked, recalling one of her old lines she used on Taaz in high school.

"Kecia, I'm serious."

"Yeah, I know," she sighed, "you're right, but I really do need to lose weight."

"Well, do it because *you* wanna do it, not because somebody else wants you to."

"To be honest, I've been trying to lose weight for years, but all of these diets aren't working for me."

"Well, you don't have to give up every food you love."

He called. "Ah, waitress," she quickly came to the table. "Ah, bring us a slab of ribs, a large root beer, some ranch, and some bacon bits for her salad...real bacon...I don't want none of that imitation stuff."

The waitress smiled, "Okay, will do,"

He nodded and she rushed to another table.

Taaz looked at Kecia. "You're gonna eat and you're gonna stop yourself when you know you've had enough… What's that crazy stuff my momma used to say around Thanksgiving? Umm…oh yea, 'People eat to get full, but only turkeys are stuffed."

"What?" Kecia laughed.

"Hey, I didn't say it."

Kecia smiled at him, "I know what you both meant," she bit her bottom lip, "Okay."

He stared at her, and quickly looked down and started rubbing his stomach, "I don't know. I'm hungry as hell; I might eat up that slab by my damn self."

"You eat too much, you might end up looking like me."

"Well, if I do, it won't matter"

She looked at him strangely. "You're being awfully nice to me. You don't have some life threatening illness, do you?"

He shook his head, "No, Kecia."

"Well, you're not turning gay on me, are you?"

His eyes grew wide and he came closer. He placed his hand on his chest. In a feminine voice, he said. "Girl, who told you? Alonzo?"

Kecia started laughing. Even though Taaz knew how to get on Kecia's last nerve, she had always loved his sense of humor.

CHAPTER 24

"Uh, those two making love was the last thing I wanted to visualize tonight," Laila said as she and Alonzo strolled up her walkway.

Alonzo bit his lip, "Well, what better way to blur them out than to have sex with me?"

"What?"

Alonzo laughed, "I'm just playing," but then he looked seriously at her, "Unless you want to do it."

Laila couldn't believe what she was hearing. "No!"

He shrugged, "Well, that's fine by me."

They walked up her steps, across her porch, and stood at the front door. Laila fumbled through her purse, searching for her keys.

With the keys finally in her hand, she placed a key in the lock and turned around to find Alonzo rocking with his hands in his pockets and looking quite bashful.

"Laila, I really had a nice time with you tonight," Alonzo said batting his eyes, mimicking a teenage girl.

Laila couldn't help but to laugh, "You are so crazy."

"But for real though, I really enjoyed our date and I sincerely hope we can continue seeing one another."

She smiled, "I enjoyed our date too."

"You really need to be with someone who makes you smile."

"And you think *you* can be the one?"

"Girl, what are you talking about? I know I'm the one."

"You know that weak game isn't going to work on me."

"Laila, I'm not about games anymore. When it comes to you, I'm *all* about the truth. Laila," he gently grabbed her waist and pulled her closer, "all bullshit aside, I want you and I want to know you inside out. If you'll give me the chance to show you how I've changed, I promise I can make you happy."

She played along with him. "Really?"

"Yes, I can make you feel like no man has or ever will."

She smiled once again and shook her head.

"You don't believe me?"

"Not really."

"Well, watch this."

He pulled her against his warm member and passionately kissed her for what seemed like eternity. She didn't want to enjoy kissing Alonzo, but his lips were a succulent delight like fresh honeydew. The kiss was soft and sensual and she gave in. Then, they finally let go.

"I bet you your spine is tingling and the rest your body is quivering…" he licked his lips, "…all over."

"No, it isn't and don't kiss me again."

"Okay, I'm sorry for crossing the line like that, but I had to at least try. Well, if you need anything and I mean anything, I'll be at Redwood Apartments, Unit 5C."

"I know where you live."

"Okay or you can call; you still have my number, right?"

"It's saved in my phone."

"Well, alright. Goodnight."

He kissed her on the cheek. He looked back at her and smiled, then walked to his car as Laila went into the house.

Soon, Laila was walking down the hall in a violet satin

Chinese robe and violet house shoes. She was sipping green tea and smiling, replaying the highlight of her night --the kiss-- over and over in her mind. A knock on the door interrupted her thoughts; she smiled and placed her mug on the coffee table and rushed to open the door.

"I knew you'd be ba-," she stopped in her tracks when she saw his face, "Quinton?"

"Where is he?"

He brushed past her.

"I don't know. Do you see a Range Rover or Mercedes outside? What do *you* want?"

"I want to know why in the hell are you trying to get back at me by sleeping with my best man."

She closed the door.

"I'm not trying to get back at you."

"So you're telling me that you're genuinely attracted to Alonzo now when you didn't give a damn about him in high school?" She heard loud thunder outside and it caught her off guard.

"Quinton," she started.

"You told me that you wanted *me*, that you were in love with *me*. Now, you're walking around holding hands with my best man? How low can you seep? You sleep with me, then my best man … Hell, you might as well go down my whole line of groomsmen. You want me to make you a damn list? Fuck them all and see if I give a fuck!"

"Hey!" Laila raised her voice, "Don't come in my house, cursing at me, insinuating that I'm some whore. You are the only one I slept with."

"Oh, you and Alonzo expect me to believe that?"

She calmed. "Yes, you are the only person in your wedding party I've slept with," she lowered her head, feeling ashamed. "I didn't sleep with the groomsmen or the best man. I slept with the groom of all people!"

"You two are lying," he shook his head, "I've always thought you were different, but now I realize-"

"Realize what, Quinton?"

"You're just like every other woman I've met," he sighed, "You know what? I'm glad I'm marrying Melanie because she's nothing like you. She wouldn't stoop as low as you," he let out a sigh of relief, "Woo, I almost made the biggest mistake of my life. I was about to end it with Melanie and be with you, but thank you for opening my eyes."

Laila gasped, "*I* haven't done anything."

"And *I* don't believe you," then he came close to her ear, "Now, if you'll excuse me I'm about to make love to the beautiful woman I'm going to spend the rest of my life with, so you and Alonzo can kiss my black ass."

He left her speechless as he walked around her and slammed the door behind him. Thunder sounded loudly until the vibrations felt as if it was pounding against her heart. Tears fell from her eyes. She began to breathe heavily and anger soon encompassed her body.

Laila marched out of the door behind him. "No, you don't get to walk out on me."

He quickly looked around at her.

"You've been out of my life for eight years and you think you can come back and control what I do when you're sleeping with my best friend and when you're about to marry her in just a few days? You didn't give a fuck about me back then and you don't now. I'm just a piece of ass you finally conquered. Then, you've got the nerve to come to my home and curse me out like you're some big shit."

Quinton looked at her in shock, surprised that she used such choice words with him.

"Quinton Harris, you keep messing with me, I'ma show you that I'm not the one you wanna mess with."

He smirked, "What are you gonna do? Tell Melanie? Go ahead. She won't believe you."

He walked on to his Yukon. She walked back in her house and slammed her door. She folded her arms and looked around the room. She started shaking her legs and her lips were quivering. She started nodding her head, looking unstable. Her cold enveloped heart became a furnace. Quinton had brought her to the point that she was about to explode.

CHAPTER 25

As her car sped along the highway, she couldn't believe what she was doing. Could she possibly end the life she worked so hard to have? Could she ruin the person she worked so hard to maintain? Could a man drive her to utter insanity and darkness? Sometimes a good woman does bad things. When it comes to a man, a woman's sense of sound judgment goes completely out of the window.

The weather grew worse by the minute, but she no longer cared. She parked her car along the curb across from an apartment complex. It started drizzling mists of rain. She was glad that she was already wearing a trench coat. She placed her keys in the pocket of her coat and grabbed an umbrella. After she locked her car doors, she made her way across the street in search for Unit 5C. Soon, she was standing at Alonzo's door. The rain started to pour, thunder sounded, and lightning lit up the sky. She placed her white and clear umbrella by the door. As soon as she heard him approaching the door, she pulled off her trench coat and threw it on top of her umbrella.

"Who is it?"

"Me." she touched her head to make sure her hairstyle was intact. Her hair was still pinned up and her red chopsticks were still in place.

"Me? Do you have a name other than *Me*?"

She waited to respond, hoping to add anticipation to his curiosity.

"Why don't you open the door and find out?" she said in a deep, sultry tone.

The door opened slowly. He peeped out and quickly pulled it open. His eyes grew wide. He was surprised to see Laila standing in his doorway wearing nothing but an extremely short satin red Chinese robe with fancy gold embroidery and red stilettos with straps tied around her leg.

Alonzo looked to the ceiling as if he was speaking to God. He bowed and said, "*Xie Ni.*" *Thank you* in Chinese.

Alonzo was looking delicious. He was wearing a white muscle shirt and charcoal gray lounge pants. She could tell he had just hopped out of the shower. He smelled fresh and Laila was pleased not to smell a single hint of Curve. Scents of Suave, a word that typically portrayed his persona, and cologne aroused her nostrils.

He stared at her in awe.

"Damn girl. Come in."

She walked in seductively, swaying her hips with each step. She felt like a beautiful top model getting ready for her photo shoot at an exotic location.

I wish I could feel this way every day.

He closed the door behind him and stared at her.

"Um, um, um. Girl, what are you-"

She placed her finger on his lips, "Shhh."

Laila didn't want to think. She didn't want to be rational. All she wanted was comfort and solidarity. She pushed him against the door and kissed him passionately. She loved how fresh his mouth tasted.

He was surprised at first but didn't protest in opposition. He just let her take over. She placed her hand under his shirt, running her fingers across his firm six-pack. She grasped his hard penis. She pulled down his pants and he quickly stepped out of them. She pulled off his muscle shirt and started back kissing him. He ran his hands up her legs and smiled when he discovered she wasn't wearing any panties. She ran her soft, delicate hands over his body. His hard member arose from the slit in his boxers. She wrapped her leg around his waist and he slipped right in with no protest from her yearning vagina. Laila was enthralled. He fit her perfectly like two missing pieces of a puzzle were finally placed together and made whole. As soon as she felt him completely within her body…knowing that it was him, looking into his beautiful brown eyes, kissing him, and touching him…she came.

"Damn girl," he moaned as she started grinding him against the door.

With endless kisses, he picked her up and carried her to his bedroom.

He laid her down on his bed and stared at her.

"Wait right there," he held his forefinger up like he was afraid she may change her mind and run away at any minute. She looked at her reflection in the mirror. Then, she noticed the countless rows of cologne bottles on his dresser.

He rushed under his bed, pulled out a plastic box full of condoms, and placed it on his nightstand. *At least, he has some sensibility left in him,* she smiled. Then he picked up his remote. He stood around the bed and he pointed his remote towards his window. She looked over to see a huge stereo system. Then, Avant's *Makin' Good Love* flooded the room. She shook her head and laughed. Avant had always been Alonzo's favorite singer since high school.

"Really?"

On the bed, Laila stood up on her knees, let her hair down and threw the chopsticks on the floor. The two started back kissing. He held her head, running his fingers through her hair. She traced kisses from his neck to his chest to his abdomen. Then, she ran her tongue back up the center of his torso and kissed him softly on the lips.

He looked at her, then he pulled the red belt loose and the robe became undone and revealed all of her. He gazed in awe like she was a great work of art, then he ran his fingers across her shoulders and pulled her robe off. He gently traced soft kisses on her shoulders. Then, he laid her on the bed, kissing her. He traced his kisses from her mouth to her neck. He made sure to place kisses all over her body. He ran his tongue across her cheek and took her breasts in his mouth. Taking his time, gently sucking. He kissed her flat abdomen. Then, he spread her legs apart and kissed her thighs. Then, he kissed her in between her legs. He hesitated, thought for a moment, and gazed up at her. He looked back down and shrugged, "Fuck it."

He licked her. Laila tried her best to compose herself but she came once again.

Alonzo grabbed a magnum and was soon on top of Laila. She wrapped her arms around him and stared him in the eyes. He entered her and moved in a slow rhythmic motion. Then, she started grinding against him in the same motion. Then, he went deeper and harder like he wanted to prove that he was the best she'll ever have.

"Harder," she whispered. He obeyed.

"Umm, you feel so good."

She clenched her walls around him and he quickly pulled out.

"Naw, you ain't bout to get off that easy."

She smiled and he quickly slid back into her. She let out a deep sigh.

"We're going all night." he said, then asked, "Can you handle me for that long?"

"I'm down to do whatever with you."

He chuckled, then stared at her. He kissed her and focused on giving her hard, quick strokes. Sweat began to pour down his body. He pulled back a little and stopped. "You gon' let me get you in the shower too?"

"Will you shut up?"

He smiled and went as deep as he could in her. Soon,

the sound of the rain flooded the room as they indulged in one another in every possible way.

CHAPTER 26

Quinton was driving down the highway in a heavy downpour. He was flipping through his playlist until *J.E. Mixes* appeared on his radio screen. He pressed the forward button multiple times until he reached number four. Then, the car blasted with *Walked out of Heaven*. At that moment, he could relate to Jagged Edge. He started singing along with the first verse.

The downpour became worse and his wipers began to fail him. He switched to high beams. He leaned forward, so he could get a better view of the highway. He noticed a car on the side of the road and a petite black woman standing in the rain.

"What the . . ."

He slowed down and the woman was shaking in fear and coldness. He let down the window and finally recognized her.

"Marla?"

"Quinton," she let out a sigh of relief.

She rushed to his window.

"You don't know how glad I am to see you," she gestured towards her tan Malibu, "My car quit on me. I had got out to check under the hood and accidentally locked my keys in the car."

"Dang, you couldn't call anybody?"

"No, my phone never has service in this area."

"Dang girl," he leaned over and opened his passenger's side door. "Hop in and get out of the rain."

She climbed into the SUV and closed the door, "Thank you."

"Let me help you ge-" He reached to open his door.

"No, I just want to go home. It's the same place I've always lived."

"Okay," he said as he drove back onto the road. She pulled off her coat and he handed her a blue blanket from his backseat.

"Thank you," she wrapped it around her.

"So," he swallowed, "you still live with your mother?"

"It's more like she lives with me because she gave me the house when she moved to San Diego. I've just been taking care of her ever since she got sick. Her man couldn't deal with her illness, so he sent her back down here."

"Oh, I'm sorry to hear that."

"It's fine. She's strong."

"Yea, Ms. Maureen has always been a fighter. She'll come out of this healthier than before."

She smiled and glanced out of the window.

"So wedding bells will be chiming for you soon, eh?"

He smirked, "Don't remind me."

"You're getting cold feet already?"

"Naw, Melanie's just been driving me crazy trying to have the perfect wedding."

"You're crazy alright over juggling her and her friend."

"What? How'd you-"

"I saw the way you were looking at her and chasing her in the store the other day."

"Oh naw, it's not what you think."

"Aw, I know you, Quinton. You've always wanted what you can't have. Once you get it, you either find out it's not what you thought it would be or don't know what to do afterwards, so you just run away."

He blew his breath, "It's sad to say, but I think you're right."

"Oh, I know I'm right."

"That's one thing about you and me; we've always understood each other."

"Yep. Good communication and bad sex."

"Aw, come on now. I wasn't that bad."

"Wasn't that bad? You were like the Energizer Bunny. You kept going and going, and after it was over, I *still* needed batteries."

"Damn."

She started laughing, "I'm just playing; you know we used to always joke like that."

"That was cold, Marla. Give me a break; we were teenagers just starting out. I'm an intelligent, hard-working man now. Sex with me is mind-blowing."

"Mind-blowing, huh? Guess that's good for you and your *wife*."

They pulled up to her house. "Wow, this place is just how I remember it."

"Yep."

"The porch swing, where we had our first kiss…that damn ceramic frog that I tripped on."

Marla laughed. "We moved it over a little, but I'll never forget that. You fell hard too, straight into the bushes."

He chuckled. "Don't remind me." He looked at her. "Marla, don't worry about your car. I'm about to call my uncle and he'll pull it to the shop.

"Thanks Quinton."

"We go way back. It's the least I can do."

CHAPTER 27

Laila went to work with a huge smile on her face. Most of her co-workers mentioned that she had a glow. She was even more talkative to the tellers, telling one how beautiful her hair was, the other about her beautiful dress, and she noticed another employee's new glasses.

She was sitting in her office typing on her computer, still smiling. That night made her a changed woman. She wore her hair down to work. That was exactly what she needed to get her mind off Quinton and Melanie. She didn't really know where she and Alonzo stood. Would things be awkward between them now? She woke up at 4 in the morning with his arms wrapped protectively around her as if he was afraid she would slip away and she did just that. She carefully removed his arms, got dressed, and left. She wanted to avoid the whole awkward morning after and she didn't want to risk someone knocking on his door and discovering her.

When Laila came back from lunch, she was surprised to find a bouquet of lilies sitting in a glass vase on her desk. "Wow, no one has ever had flowers delivered to me," she looked at the card. It read:

Simply thinking of you.
—Alonzo

She smiled. It was 3pm; she had one hour left until it was time to go home. Thursdays especially towards the end of the month were typically slow days. Most of the employees had gone for the day. It was only Laila; the loan officer, Ana-Leigh; the receptionist, Heather; the teller, Audrey; and the drive-thru teller, Ms. Bobbie.

Laila received a knock on her door; she looked up to see Alonzo, standing in the doorway, looking debonair in a gray suit and a light blue collared shirt underneath.

"Good Afternoon, I came to apply for a private loan."

"By all means, come in,"

He entered and closed the door behind him. He sat in the chair across from her.

"So I missed you this morning."

"Yeah, I had some things I needed to do,"

"Umm, you don't know what you missed,"

She looked confused, "What *I* missed?"

"I was going to fix you breakfast in bed."

"Oh really, how romantic," she typed an entry into her computer, "Maybe you can next time."

His brows raised, "So there will be a next time," he smiled.

"Aw, you tricked me," Laila wrinkled her nose.

"Well, you know last night came as a shock to me."

"Yeah, it was a shock to me too."

"Because I've been trying to get you for like damn...almost fifteen years."

"Umm huh."

"So any regrets?"

"Umm...no, it was nice," she exhaled, "Very nice."

"Oh, it was... huh?" he licked his lips. He pulled off his coat and placed it on the chair next to him. Laila finally looked at him and gave him a strange glare. He got up and locked her door and closed her blinds.

"Whoa…whoa…wait a minute. What are you doing?" she quickly arose and came around her desk.

"What does it look like I'm doing?" he asked pulling off his tie.

"Alonzo, no," she said as he placed his hand on her hand. She pushed him back, keeping her hand on his chest.

"Aw come on. Be adventurous."

"No, you're not going to make me lose my job."

"Aw, please, you and the owners go way back. They can't afford to let you go."

"Alonzo," she said pushing him back once more.

"Okay, okay. I'm sorry. You said no. I should respect that," he looked apologetically into her eyes. She finally dropped her hand.

"I just dropped by to see you and let you know we're cool. You don't have to avoid me or start back acting all shy and timid or mean again."

"Oh okay, but I wasn't planning on doing that anyway."

His eyes widened, "Really?"

She nodded and he smiled.

"So, uh, I'll see you tonight at the rehearsal?"

"Um…yeah, you will,"

They kept staring at each other. Laila's heart began to race. He gently grasped and caressed her hand and slowly pulled her towards him. He wrapped his arms around her and held her for a while. He wore a different type of cologne and Laila became indulged in the enticing, sensual smell. She closed her eyes and grasped his back tightly with her fingers pressing his back. She deeply inhaled his fragrance once more.

"Umm, what is that cologne you're wearing?"

"Dolce and Gabbana Light Blue."

She was drawn by the alluring scent far more than Curve. Alonzo began rubbing her back, then he slowly made his way down and grasped her behind with both hands and pulled her against him. The two pulled away just enough to gaze into each other's eyes. He began to gently hold her waist and brought one hand up to her face. He gently caressed her face.

Laila breathed heavily, gazing from his eyes to his lips.

He panted, "You're so damn beautiful."

He pressed his lips against hers, then they started wildly tongue-kissing each other. He pushed the items on her desk back. She gave him a puzzled look. He picked her up and sat her on the desk. Before she could protest, he kissed her again. He lifted her hips and slid her nude lace panties down, balled them up and put them in his pocket. She wrinkled her brows. He pulled the office chair closer to her and sat down. Laila leaned back, placing her hands on her desk to keep her upright. He buried his face in between her legs, paying close attention to her clit. He stared at her intensely as he savored her. She arched her back. She wanted to moan but didn't want to risk her co-workers hearing her. She murmured.

"You like that huh?"

She nodded.

Her lips were trembling and her spine was tingling just as Alonzo had described she would be. She felt lightheaded and hot. She could feel her juices running down her leg. Alonzo ran his tongue down her thighs, never taking his eyes off her. He stood up and Laila quickly hopped up. He grabbed her and kissed her once again.   Breathing heavily, he quickly unbuckled his pants and lifted up her skirt. He pressed her back against the adjacent wall next to her co-worker, Matthew Keegan's office. She was glad that he was out of the office. Soon, Alonzo was deep within her, making her climb that very wall. She did not want to object. She loved feeling that same rush she felt the night before.

CHAPTER 28

Later that night, everyone but Laila, Gia, and Kecia was at the church for the final rehearsal.

"I'm glad y'all came out tonight," Quinton said to his boys. "Mom wanted to see us rehearse but this is the only night she could come."

Carol looked around the church. "Boy, this looks just like our church, Quinton,"

"Yes, I said the same thing,"

"And y'all paid all of this money to have it at the white folks' church, when you could have had it at our own church for free?"

"I know, but this is what Melanie wants,"

"Well, I know for a fact that the 22nd is still available, so you can still chan-"

Melanie interrupted, "We could, but this church has beautiful outdoor scenery. The backdrop of the church is impeccable. Our wedding photos will be absolutely breathtaking."

"Oh, I had my wedding at my church and the pictures came out just fine," she smirked, "but hey, now we're divorced, so maybe you know best." Carol eyed her with cynicism as she made her way down the center aisle.

Quinton followed behind her. She stopped to talk to Alonzo, Taaz, and David.

"Alonzo, did you ever think you'll see the day Quinton settle down?"

"Naw, I was very shocked when he told me. He kept that from me real good."

"When are you gonna settle down?"

"Oh, I'm ready, just waiting for the right woman to come along."

"Right," Carol pursed her lips.

"Oh, don't worry, Ma. He's next in line. I've spent hours practicing my swing, so the garter can land right in his hand at the reception," Carol smiled and walked on to Aunt Judy.

"Whatever man, you better sling that to Taaz."

"The hell he will," Taaz said.

"Yeah, throw it Taaz," Alonzo joked, "and get Melanie to throw her bouquet to Kecia. Then, you two will be getting it in on the dance floor."

"Ugh, naw, y'all play too much."

"Aw yea, I like that. Taaz can clench the garter between his teeth and kiss Kecia's beautiful thick chocolate thighs as he inches up her leg."

He gagged, "I think I'm 'bout to be sick, man," He held his stomach and he walked off.

"You know you lovesick, man,"

They started laughing and high-fiving. The front door of the church slowly opened. Gia, Kecia, and Laila entered.

They began the rehearsal. The entire night, Laila and Alonzo could not keep their eyes off one another. Quinton became jealous. When the two were adjacent from each other at the altar, Quinton stepped in front of Alonzo, so the two could not see each other. After practice, one of the bridesmaids approached Alonzo.

"Laila, tell me you didn't sleep with Alonzo," Kecia said. The girls knew Alonzo's *I hit dat* look all too well.

"What? No," Laila's eyes grew wide and her nose

twitched.

"Oh my God. You did sleep with him," Kecia said in shock.

Gia nodded and smiled. "Now that's what I'm talking about."

"Laila, what were you thinking?"

She sighed, "I was thinking I needed to move on from *you know who*."

Kecia shook her head, "Uh, you are-"

"My hero," Gia finished.

"More like a slut."

"Kecia, I can't believe you said that," Laila said.

"Forget her. There's nothing wrong with what you're doing. Men, do it every single day."

Kecia cut her eyes at Gia.

"Laila, I don't know what's gotten into you…"

"Some dick," Gia mumbled under her breath while pretending to cough.

Kecia cut her eyes at Gia then firmly looked at Laila. "But I'm warning you. You need to stop this right now before it all hits the fan."

The bridesmaid was still trying to get Alonzo's attention, but his mind was elsewhere.

"Hey, I was wondering, would you like to go out tonight? We could go out to dinner and drop by my place."

She gets closer, but he is staring at Laila walking to the lobby. "I have a Jacuzzi."

"Women still use that line?"

"Excuse me?" she wrinkled her brows.

Laila stopped in the doorway and looked at Alonzo. She tilted her head, signaling him to come with her.

"Hello?" she said attempting to get his attention again, "Quinton thought we might hit it off, so I'm just trying to see wha--"

"Yeah, you know what? I gotta go. Talk to David though," he rushed down the aisle and stopped to talk to

David and Taaz.

"So we gon' play Spades again tonight, man?" Taaz asked.

"Yea, we can do that," David said.

"You coming Lonzo?"

"Naw, not tonight," Alonzo said, "Ah David, Q's cousin wanna holla at you."

"Um, well alright," David looked towards her. He rushed on past them.

"Slow down, boy. That pussy ain't going nowhere," Taaz called after him.

***

Kecia walked down the sidewalk with a smile on her face. She made no mention of her anniversary to her girls since she knew they cared nothing for her and Leonard's relationship.

"Hey baby," she called.

She entered and saw the place lit with candles and a bouquet of red roses already in the vase on the center of her dining table. She sighed in relief.

"Finally."

Leonard appeared from the kitchen.

"Hey, what took you so long?"

"I was picking up your gift from Mama's. You know I had to hide it from you. So here baby," she handed him a black box with a silver bow on it. He smiled and quickly opened it.

"A Rolex. Thank you baby," he leaned over and kissed her. He placed the watch on the table and held her hand.

"Now close your eyes," he led her down the hall and into the guest bedroom. He stepped in front of her and got down on one knee.

"Open them."

She gasped. "You're propos-"

"Ta da."

He gestured behind him and she looked up.

"A treadmill?"

"Don't you like it?"

"Leonard, it's our anniversary. We're supposed to give each other something personal."

"Baby, I spent $600 on this treadmill. It's the Horizon Fitness T101. It's to help you work on yourself. You can't get more personal than that."

"Yes, you can. I bought you that damn watch for $899.52. I thought you were going to give me jewelry too. I've been giving you subtle hints all this month."

"Jewelry? You have enough jewelry. This is something that you *actually* need."

She gasped.

"No you didn't," she stormed out of the room.

"Kecia wait."

He followed her down the hall.

"No, the hell this motherfucker didn't. I'm so over this," she grabbed his gift from the table and marched to the window.

"Kecia, what are you doing?"

She lifted up the window and tossed the box out.

"Why did you do that?"

"Get out."

"Can't we discuss this?"

"We can when you get back, but now I don't even want to look at you. The treadmill will be out on the curb in the morning. Have fun on your business trip."

"Kecia, I'm sorry. I had a special evening for us planned."

"Get out!" she repeated as she opened her door.

"Kecia, please," he said, "Let's discuss this over dinner."

"Ta, since you think I'm too fat, I ain't finna eat with yo' ass."

He sighed and walked out. "But I cooked asparagus for you."

"Does it look like I eat some damn asparagus?"

She slammed the door in his face.

CHAPTER 29

Laila was in a particularly good mood. She decided to give the alcohol a rest and stay away from her cold, uninviting dining room table. She decided to actually *live* in her living room. A room she once was bent on calling a show room much like her patio/lanai. She decided to take a page out of Kecia's book and crank up the air, so it could feel like a cold winter's night. She threw on a big gray sweater and sweat pants and her favorite pink socks with purple hearts on them. She made a cup of hot cocoa and got cozy on her plush white sofa. She never knew her couch would feel so good. She wrapped her blanket around her.

She turned on her television and started watching the movie, *The Lake House*.

A movie about a man and a woman who fall in love yet lived two years apart. One in the present. One in the past.

Quinton's moving on with his life, making Melanie his present and future while Laila was living in the past, still in love with an 18-year-old boy. If only she could write a letter like Sandra Bullock and Keanu Reeves to change the course of time.

Alonzo seemed to be her remedy. Being with him felt

good and took her mind completely off Quinton. She finally understood why so many women were taken by Alonzo. He was funny and quite the charmer. He was undeniably attractive and utterly knew how to satisfy a woman. She smiled as she thought of their hot passionate escapades. It was an exhilarating mind-blowing rush that she could not wait to experience again.

Her phone rang and she answered, never turning her head from the screen. Since the only person who had started calling her during that time of night was Alonzo, she assumed it was him.

She said, "I'm glad you made it home safely."

"So you really did it?"

"Who is this?"

He ignored her question. "You slept with Alonzo after I left last night."

"Quinton," she said, "Hmm, so Alonzo has been spreading our business to his friends."

"He didn't have to."

"So you were following me?"

"No, I didn't follow you," she sighed, "David lives in the apartment right across the yard from him. All they did was look out of the window and saw your half-naked ass waiting at his door. Taaz said you were looking like a red China doll."

She laughed slightly. "Taaz is crazy."

"Laila, this is not the time. I talked with Alonzo; he said you never intended on sleeping with him, but all of a sudden, you show up at his place?" He cleared his throat, "Did I push you to sleep with him after I came over last night?"

"I- I guess," she turned off the television and sighed. "In a way you did. You insulted me and mangled whatever dignity I had left. I almost went crazy when you made me picture you in bed with Melanie or any woman, but me. I had to get that image out of my head, so that's when I…" she searched for the right words to say, "inanely paid

Alonzo a visit."

Quinton sighed heavily, which sounded like static in her ear.

"Quinton, why did you think I was sleeping with Alonzo?"

"I don't know. I thought you two were lying when we ran into you on the square."

"Well, I honestly had no intentions of ever being with Alonzo, of all people, under any circumstance."

He sighed. "I'm sorry I went off like that. I shouldn't have come at you like that. I'm with Melanie; I can't control who you spend your time with. I- I hope that we can at least be friends again."

"I don't know, Quinton. This is a complicated situation that we're in."

"Yes, it is," he paused, "Do you actually like Alonzo?"

"I- I don't know. I'm just confused right now."

"Yeah, I know the feeling," he said, "I thought after our argument last night, I was finally over you; I could finally move on. After we had sex, I thought I could finally stop wondering, *what if*, but I just can't get you off my mind."

"Oh, well I can't-"

A knock on her door interrupted her.

"I have to go," she quickly hung up and turned off her phone. She rushed to the door and opened it, expecting Alonzo, but to her surprise it was –

"Melanie?" Laila's heart started racing. Melanie's eyes were bloodshot, and tears poured down her cheeks.

She sobbed, "I think Quinton is having an affair."

"An affair? Wha-Wha-Wha…" Laila stuttered, afraid that Melanie was about to figure out that she was the one who slept with Quinton, "What makes you think that?"

"He's been acting strange, making secret phone calls, and sneaking off. I even caught him going through my phone."

"Really?"

So that's how he got my number.

"Like he's trying to see if I'm talking to other men and men who are guilty of infidelity are insecure like that."

"No," Laila pretended to be shocked.

"Girl, we haven't had sex since we've been in town."

"Really? I thought you two did last night."

"No, I was eager for it, but he snuck off somewhere, talking about he forgot to run an errand for his mom *at midnight*, Laila," she looked at her.

"Well, he's always been a Momma's Boy."

Melanie ignored Laila's comment and paced back and forth, her mind still racing. Her hands were on her hips and she looked at the floor as if the answer could be found within Laila's house, "I bet you he's been messing around with one of his old girlfriends from high school."

Laila, who was sitting on the arm of her loveseat, adjusted herself. Her eyes grew wide, and her heart raced more rapid than ever.

"I bet you it's that Marla Gomillion. I saw the way she was eyeing him at the store. Or…"

Laila knew the only way to cloud Melanie's suspicion was to bring the focus on Melanie herself. She cleared her throat, "Um, maybe there's a reasonable explanation for his behavior. Maybe he's planning a surprise for you."

"Did he tell you something?"

She tried to think of a lie, "No, bu- but Alonzo has been um… working with him on um…something, but they uh… won't tell me in fear of me giving it away, I presume."

Laila hoped Melanie believed her.

"Really?" she hugged her, "Thank you for helping me get these negative thoughts out of my mind."

"Oh, it's no problem," Laila sighed in relief.

Melanie noticed Laila's bowl of popcorn and hot cocoa. "Hey, this looks like fun. Can I spend the night with you? We can have a slumber party for old time's sake."

"Uh, sure. Why not?"

"Okay, let me get my bags," she made her way to the door and let out a sigh of relief.

Her bags? Oh, so she just knew I was going to say yes. Well, at least, she doesn't know about Quinton and me.

Melanie exhaled. "That eases my mind completely. I thought I was going to have to cut a bitch," she joked.

"No, we wouldn't want that."

Laila rubbed her neck as she followed Melanie out of the door.

CHAPTER 30

Quinton was walking down the sidewalk on the square. He had been struggling with his feelings about Laila and Melanie while also trying to deal with Alonzo. The wedding had been stressing him but more than anything, his career plans were on his mind. Once the wedding was out of the way, he wanted to already have a firm plan on what he'd doing.

He spotted Marla coming out of Gia's salon.

"Hi Marla."

"Oh hi Quinton," she looked surprised to see him. "Thanks for getting my car out of the shop. You didn't have to do that."

"It's the least I could do. You helped me a lot in high school."

"I sure did, didn't I?" she looked around, "To dish out money like that, you must be doing very well for yourself."

A car passed and someone beeped at Quinton. He waved.

"Yeah, something like that. Right now, I'm in the process of starting my own company."

"Ta...well, good for you," she smirked and shook her

head. She was not impressed.

"What?"

"Nothing."

"I know that look, Marla," he said, "What do you have to say?"

"Umm…well, let me ask you this. How many times have you been promoted at your current job?"

"Once,"

"Once?" Marla shook her head, "so you just want to jump from manager to CEO just like that?"

"So you think I'm not ready?"

"I'm no expert, but I don't expect to be running Wal-Mart any time soon. I think you should stay where you are."

"Humph…you sound like Melanie."

Marla raised her brows and frowned.

"She doesn't want me to start my own business."

"I'm not saying you should never own one. I am saying you need to grow and learn more about the business. Gain all of the knowledge and experience you can, then go after that dream."

"Marla, you just don't know the hell they put me through,"

"Well, I face hell every day at my job and I'm going to stay until God moves me from that situation with a new opportunity. So, if you're not meant to be with your company, then they'll fire you or lay you off. If they don't realize their mistake and try to get you back, then you should move on to other companies."

Quinton was amazed at how Marla was giving him advice about his job and he never told her what happened.

He thought, *Once Hearst realized the mistake that was made, he immediately called to rehire me.*

"And if the other companies don't want your ass, then you have no choice. It leads you to building a company from the ground up," she continued.

He was confused. *She wants me to start a company only if I can't keep a job?*

She went on, "Now, if the company keeps you and continues to promote you, then one day, you'll be ready for that business. Who knows? God may even give you a business that is already fully operating and it may be that very same company. Then, all you have to do is apply your skills and make it your own."

"Hmm…that makes a lot of sense," he nodded, "I never thought about it that way." Quinton was deep in concentration. Marla could tell something was going on at his job.

"If you're facing that much stress at work, why are you even trying to get married right now and to a girl, you gon' divorce quicker than Kim Kardashian?"

"Aw, I see you got jokes. The wedding plans were already set, my work issues just kinda popped up."

"You know when you don't make the right decisions, everything in life seems to be turned upside down," Marla sighed. "That's our problem: we're always rushing to get married, get a new job, and have children. We do what our minds and other people tell us, but we never listen to our hearts." She seemed distant.

He studied her disposition. She finally looked back at him. "You know if you lose your job, you gon' lose Melanie even though she ain't got one."

"Got what? A job?"

"Umm…huh."

"She has a job and she's not like that, honestly."

"Right."

"We've been talking about my dreams, but I'm surprised you're not following your dreams. You wanted to go to college and double major in dance and business administration."

"Wow, I'm surprised you remembered."

"Of course, I remember,"

"I commuted to college for a little while, but I dropped out my sophomore year when my mother got sick… I don't care what anyone says; my mother is always going to come first."

"I heard that. That's a noble thing you're doing; some people wouldn't want to be bothered. I know I would take care of my mother if anything happened to her."

"Yeah, I know you would take care of Ms. Carol, *Momma's Boy*."

"So you have jokes once again?"

"Umm huh," she said. His phone buzzed. He quickly pulled it out and sent a text.

"So which girl are you toying with today?"

"What?"

"Oh, don't think I don't know. Gia told me all about your Melanie and Lana love triangle… No, Laila is her name, right?"

"Yeah, that's it," he sighed, "I don't know what got into me… I just… I just wasn't thinking right in the head."

"No, you weren't thinking with the right one," she quickly glanced at his crouch, rolled her eyes, and looked back at him, "You better make a decision before it comes back to bite you."

Dang, Marla knows me like a book.

"What would you do?"

"Me personally? If I was a guy, I wouldn't be with either one of those shallow women because all they think about is looks, sex, and money. They act like Alexandra and her clique did back in high school times ten."

"Naw, they're not that bad."

"Well, I'll take your word for it," she thought, "Umm…you should do what I did in high school."

"And what's that?"

"When I picked between you and Alonzo, I made a list."

"Hold up. Alonzo tried to get with you too?"

"Come on now. It's Alonzo. Who didn't he try to get with?"

"Well, can't argue with that."

"As I was saying, Alonzo was eyeing me, but then you decided that you wanted to make us work again. So, I made a list of likes and dislikes and you beat Alonzo by a long shot. Come to think of it, I only listed dislikes for Alonzo. His looks were the only like."

"What didn't you like about me?"

"It may sound ironic, but it was the simple fact that whenever you're in a relationship, you're always longing to be with someone else. Like, when we were together, you wanted Laila, Shawna, Latoya, Jasmine …shoot, the list goes on. When you had other girlfriends, there you were trying to get back with me …Carmen …oh and Shardae. Those facts made me come to this conclusion: you, Quinton Harris, have never really been in love."

"You and your theories," Quinton shook his head, "but what makes you think that?"

Marla sighed, "Quinton, anyone who cheats on a significant other doesn't love her in the first place. It may seem like love, but if you hurt her, it's not. You didn't cheat on Melanie with some stranger; you did it with someone she loved, someone right under her nose, her best friend. Quinton, that's not love."

"So you're saying I've never been in love in my entire life?"

"Aside from yo' *momma*, that's exactly what I'm saying."

"Why is everyone telling me that?" he thought to himself.

Marla glanced at her phone. "Hey, I have to go pick my niece up from dance rehearsal."

"Well, I'm glad she's following in your footsteps."

"Yep, and I'm proud of her," she blew her breath, "Any time you want to talk, you know my number. Thanks again, Quinton," she briefly grasped his wrist in gratitude. Then, she walked down the sidewalk.

"Marla, have you ever been in love?" he called.

She looked back at him, "Once, but he didn't feel the same way."

"If you don't mind me asking, who was he?"

She shrugged. "You."

She made sure the street was clear before she walked across.

Meanwhile, Gia was busy gossiping only several feet away in her shop. The place was full of her patrons, some sitting in chairs waiting and some under the dryer. Gia and her stylists were at their stations styling hair. Gia just loved the sound of dryers, the smell of curlers smoking, the running water, the chatter, and the sound of money hitting her hands.

"Uh huh girl. I told her she was gon' need a weed eater or something to manage that tangled mess on her head."

Her stylist, Sandra, a yellow short heavyset girl with burgundy hair, glanced out of the window while she was curling her client's hair. Then she quickly looked out again, and leaned backward to get a better look.

"Gia! Girl, come look."

"What, girl?"

She walked over to her stylist's station.

"Somebody's man didn't have the balls to park in *front* of the shop."

Gia looked out of the window. She saw Leonard, getting out of one of the dealership cars, smiling. He rushed to open the door for Tacara. He held her hand as she got out. He pulled out money and gave it to her. She hugged him and gave him a big, long tongue kiss.

"Cousin my ass," she walked back to her station. "And they got the nerve to come to *my* shop?"

"He's bold as hell, ain't he, Gia?"

"I wonder why Kecia doesn't ever believe you," another stylist said.

"Love is blind, honey," an older patron said.

"Yep, but I'm going to find a way to get her to believe me even if it kills me. I need to take some kind of outrageous, drastic measure."

"Girl, you sho'll need to," Sandra agreed.

"Uh, one time they had got my man on video, showed it to me, and my dumb ass still didn't believe it was him," Sandra's customer said.

"Uh uh, girl."

"Ah, is she about to come in?" Gia asked.

Sandra leaned back again. "Naw, they're still talking."

"Ah Dedra, go turn my open sign to closed and lock the door."

Everyone started laughing as Gia's young client obeyed her orders.

"Girl, you so silly."

"And none of y'all better get up to let that ho in *my* shop."

"I heard that."

"Umm huh, we gon' treat this bitch like she's Oprah at a Hermes store."

"I don't know, Gia. If Oprah was at the door, I would have to let her in."

"I know right."

The girl approached the door and tried to pull it open. She peered into the shop and everyone looked in the opposite direction.

CHAPTER 31

Alonzo and Laila were having dinner at the local Japanese restaurant. Alonzo's phone vibrated. It read Quinton. He placed the call on silent and stuck the phone back in his pocket. Laila assumed it may be a lady friend.

"Uh, I absolutely hated your ex-girlfriend."

"You're talking about Alexandra, aren't you?" he burst out laughing.

"Yeah,"

"She gave you a hard ass time."

"Yes, she did and you never made it any better, constantly flirting with me in front of her."

"Yea, now that was some fun,"

She shook her head. "Whatever happened to her? Oh and let's not forget Gallena Riley."

"Well, they finally stopped fighting over me, and I messed around with them on and off over the years. I don't know where they are now. We kind of just stopped talking. I haven't talked to Gallena in five years, and Alexandra in about two."

"Oh, you kept in touch with them very well."

"You can say that, but it was *your* boyfriend that I

hated."

"Who Deon?" she knew Quinton didn't like him, but never Alonzo.

"Yes,"

"Why?"

"He deflowered my delicate flower. I wanted to be the first," he poked out his lip.

"Ugh, shut that up," Laila said and hit him with a Japanese egg roll.

"I see you're back to hitting me with food. Flip me the finger and it'll be just like old times.

Laila laughed, "You always had me flipping you off."

"I could always bring out the bad side of you," he licked his lips.

Laila shook her head, then remembered, "'If you throwing that at me, why you walking off with him?'" she said trying to mock him.

He looked strangely. "I said that?"

"Yes, you did."

"Oh yea, yea. We were on that senior trip and you walked off with Quinton to go up Stone Mountain."

"Yep," Laila laughed. She started to sip her sweet tea.

"Yeah, he took me up there too, but I was like, 'Naw, I ain't feelin' this, you gon' have to give me some flowers or suh'thin," Alonzo said rolling his eyes and speaking in a feminine voice. Laila laughed with tea still in her mouth, spraying Alonzo's face. She covered her mouth.

"Ugh man,"

"Oh, I'm so sorry."

"Thank you, thank you," he started wiping himself off.

"Here let me help," she got up and picked up a folded napkin. She held his face and patted. He stared at her and she got closer to him and patted each moist spot. She looked him in the eyes. They just froze, staring deeply into each other's eye and she started slowly wiping his left cheek.

She broke their gaze and eased back into her seat. She

cleared her throat.

"Well, this is a delightful outing,"

"Yes, it is," he was still staring at her. Everything grew quiet.

Alonzo licked his lips, "You know what? I know I used to play with you a lot, but I remember the first time I started liking you for real."

Laila was intrigued and gave him her undivided attention.

He continued, "In ninth grade, we were in Ms. Evans class reading Romeo & Juliet. She had you reading Juliet's lines…"

"I remember that. You would always be asleep whenever it was time for us to read aloud, but with this particular play, you were begging Ms. Evans to be Romeo."

"Yes, I was. When you read those lines, you delivered them with passion and all I could hear was you moaning as you said 'Oh Romeo.'"

"What?" Laila was amused, "Yea, she made us get up in front of the class and you tried to kiss me."

"And you slapped the hell out of me," he recalled, "I don't know those sounds from you did something to me that no girl at the school had ever did and as you know, they *did* some things."

"Uh T-M-I,"

"Sorry, but I'm just being real."

"Well, that's one thing about you, you've never sugar coated anything with me."

"Exactly. Now you've got me thinking about ninth grade year when you were a cute little nerd."

"Uh, don't remind me." Laila scrunched up her nose. She remembered Alonzo would always walk over to her desk before class began, tug her ponytail, and call her his old lady as a joke.

"But then our tenth grade year, you came back all transformed and had all the guys wanting you. They could finally see what I already saw in you."

Laila pursed his lips and glared at him. "Right."

After dinner, they decided to take a walk in the park. They strolled along the bike path and gazed up at the star filled sky.

"So, am I taking your mind off Quinton?"

"You're doing a good job, yet his name tends to come up in every conversation."

"Well, yeah…I mean he's my boy, I can't help it,"

"I understand."

"But I'll try my best not to mention him anymore."

They approached his Range Rover. He rushed over to open her door.

"Hmm, still being chivalrous. I must have really laid it on you," she teased.

He pressed against her, "You have no idea."

She smiled and leaned forward. She started kissing him passionately. She grabbed him, pushed him on the passenger seat, pulled the door in slightly and straddled him. She slammed the door. He grabbed her behind and let the seat all the way back and said, "*Konichee wa.*"

CHAPTER 32

Laila had been enjoying her dates and *sessions* with Alonzo. He managed to numb her pain and she felt she could finally handle and accept Quinton and Melanie's impending nuptials. She had been contemplating for a while, but she decided to finally confront Quinton. She woke up and put on her pink spandex Under Armour outfit that she had never worn. She decided to run a few blocks. Soon, she found herself at Quinton's childhood home. She knocked on the door and he answered with a puzzled look on his face.

"Laila, what are you doing here?"

"I- I want to talk to you."

"Good because there's something I need to tell you too."

"Okay, but let me say what I have to say first."

She walked into the living room.

"Have a seat."

"No, I'm fine right here," she looked at him, "I've been stuck in a rut for all of these years and I never knew why. I've grown to become shy, bitter, and afraid once again just like I was in high school. I thought maybe the reason was my parents, but I know now it's you. It's always been you. Not being myself, pretending to be this and that or bourgeois as the girls call it to mask how I truly felt which is alone."

"Laila-"

"I mean I waited year after year, hoping that we would bump into each other whenever you were back in town. Then, I've had failed relationship after failed relationship and a few of those men would have made great husbands, but they never measured up to you. The only thing I can be proud of is my career and I have my dear old estranged mom to thank for that since I work for her old 'boss man'."

"Just let me say wh-"

"If it wasn't for Mr. Henderson, I don't know where I would be right now," Laila said,

"Maybe lost in my life, career, and love, so Quinton… I'm here before you… right now to let you know… that I finally have the strength to let you go."

"What?"

"There's no more opposition from me; you're free to be with Melanie and have your happily ever after with her. I- I give you my blessing."

"Where is this coming from?"

"I'm…" she paused. "I'm letting you go, so *I* can finally be free." Laila felt peace come over her and like she could finally breathe. She smiled. "Free, Quinton. Free to live. Free to love. I can finally be free from waiting and free from reliving my past. Free."

"So, is Alonzo the reason for your new found revelation?"

"Alonzo?"

"Yes, you're falling for him, aren't you?"

"Oh God, no. This happened all on my own. I know now that I'm capable of loving and being loved by someone other than you. That someone may be from my past, someone I do not know and will meet in the future, or it could even be someone in my present right now. All I

175

know is that he will find me and I know now that he's not you."

"Whoa…whoa. Not me? Wait a minute. Let's discuss this. How do you know I'm not the one?"

"Because I'm not your fiancé," Laila smirked, "Quinton, I know you're not the one because you would have found me. In all of these years, you've never even looked for me or found my number from a friend of a friend. Even when you first saw Melanie two years ago, you could have gotten my address, found me, and tried to convince me to leave whoever I was with for you and I would have dropped everything I was doing and ran off to be with you. That's how bad I wanted you."

"I- I never knew you felt that way."

"Yea, I had it bad."

"But, what if I'm just now opening my eyes, Laila and I'm realizing who you are and falling in love with the woman you've become."

"*What if?* Quinton, I've lived my whole life on what ifs. 'What if Quinton wants to be with me? What if Quinton marries me instead of Melanie?"

"Laila, our chapter is not complete. What if-"

Laila shook her head. "You've made your decision. You're marrying Melanie."

"But wha-"

She couldn't believe what she was hearing. Quinton was trying to have her and Melanie.

"What ifs can't keep me warm at night, but Alonzo has been doing a good job at it lately," she could tell that mentioning Alonzo upset him, "and then one day, my dream man will come into my life and him and I will be together."

She smiled, "So, I'll see you and your wife-to-be for our double date tonight."

Quinton looked at her in disbelief and she walked out, letting the door close behind her. He just stared at the door.

"Hell naw," he grabbed his keys and rushed out.

***

Soon, Quinton was at Alonzo's door. Alonzo stared at his friend with questioning eyes yet he had an idea of what his friend of twenty-three years wanted. He was wearing blue creased slacks and an unbuttoned white long sleeved collared shirt.

"You're up and at it early, man."

"Can I talk you for a minute?"

"Yeah, just getting ready for work." He turned and Quinton followed him to his room.

Quinton sat on the bed in silence as Alonzo buttoned up his shirt and picked up his red bow tie.

He looked down at Alonzo's nightstand and saw brochures and a letter addressed to Alonzo.

"H&L?" Quinton asked, "You switched banks?"

"Yes, is that a crime?"

"Naw, but we set up accounts at BankFirst six years ago."

"Well, I thought it was time for a change."

"When did you do this?"

"About three weeks ago."

"But BankFirst is a national brand with over 64 offices and over 34 locations in Georgia alone. There's a branch in Atlanta, Savannah, and here. You spend over 60% of your work hours traveling…it just makes no sense to switch to a locally-owned bank."

"Well, what can I say? They offered me something that the other banks didn't have."

"Something or someone?"

Alonzo smirked and shook his head.

"Don't worry. I got this. I'm the Banking and Finance degree holder, remember?"

"Look man, I came over here to tell you something."

"I'm listening."

"I want you to stop seeing Laila."

"Come again?"

"You heard me."

"Now, why would I do that?" he looked in the mirror, putting on his tie. "You know what, man? You have some nerve telling me not to see a woman you've been playing games with."

"I haven't been playing games with her."

"Whatever, man. You've always known how she felt about you and used that to your advantage to get her in bed," he blew his breath, "You had your chance in high school. Now, you're about to marry her best friend, our classmate, my distant cousin, *Melanie*."

"I know everything is twisted and messed up, but-"

"You don't want me to see her," he finished.

"Yes."

"So, have you broken it off with Melanie?" he asked as he put on his black suit jacket.

"Man, you know I haven't."

"Well then, I can still see her. Come to think of it, I have to stop by my new bank and make a *deposit* before I meet with my client," he beamed as he grabbed his briefcase, "So, *we'll* see you tonight, bruh."

CHAPTER 33

Kecia was on the outside of her apartment just below her kitchen window. She was busy digging through bushes trying to find Leonard's gift.

"I don't know what the hell I was thinking. I hope I still got the receipt," she said to herself still searching through the bushes, "Oh yea, it's in my purse… I hope Jerome didn't come through and find the watch."

She heard a car horn beep and she turned around.

"I know that ass from anywhere," Gia said laughing.

"Shut up, girl," Kecia said as she kept digging through bushes and fallen leaves.

"What are you looking for?"

"Aw, I got it," Kecia picked it up and dusted it off.

Gia shook her head. "Hey, come take a ride with me," she leaned over in her seat and opened the passenger door.

"I can't. I gotta return this watch."

"Well, I can take you. You'll save on gas."

Kecia gave her a strange look. "I don't know why you're trying to lure me in your car, but I can't pass on a chance to save some gas money," she got in and closed the door.

Gia was concentrating on the road while Kecia was still looking at her strangely.

Gia finally spoke. "The other day, you asked me, what kind of friend am I? Well, I'm the type who doesn't want her *true* friend hurt by anyone. So, since you won't believe a word that comes out of my mouth, I am going to *show* you the kind of friend I am."

She pulled up to Leonard's place of employment.

"The car lot? Gia, why are we here?"

There was no response as she quickly put the car in park, turned her switch, and took out the keys.

"Just get out."

She grabbed her purse, and they both got out of the car. They began to look around the lot.

"I just want you to observe."

"Observe what? Leonard's not here."

"Ooo, a candy apple red Camaro with black stripes. I think I just found me a new man."

A white salesman in his early 20's approached them.

"Hi, my name is Dan. What can I do you for?"

Gia glared at him and frowned, "Excuse me?"

Kecia put her hand to her head.

"Um, I mean how may I help you? I see you're interested in our-"

"No, I want Leonard Thurman. Is he in today?"

"No, but I'll be more than happy to assist you in finding the car of your dreams."

"Well, this just might be *him*," she said as she rubbed the trunk.

"Well, I can get the keys and we can go for a test drive."

"You seem like an intelligent young fella. I bet you sell cars left and right getting commissions straight out the ass."

He looked confused.

"No ma'am. Actually I just-"

"But I need someone who barely gets any commissions. Someone who doesn't meet yearly quotas."

He looked confused once again.

"Who I need is Leonard Thurman, so when will he be back?"

"Ma'am, Leonard is our top salesman. No one can top him, not even our boss."

"Oh really, so where is Leonard Thurman?"

"He's on vacation."

"Vacation?" Kecia asked.

"Yeah, I think he went to Montego Bay."

"Uh huh," Kecia said.

"He said his girlfriend had family out that way."

"Really?" Kecia said.

"But I'll go get the keys and we can let you try this puppy out."

"Okay," Gia said. He walked towards the building.

Kecia shook her head, "That lying no good motherfu-"

"Ooo, this Camaro has all of the features I've been looking for."

"Ho, you can't afford that right now. Let's go."

She pulled Gia away, and they jumped in the car and sped off.

"Thanks girl. I was scared of the truth, but I needed to hear that. I knew my suspicions had been right all along."

"Well, just know I'm here for you."

"Well, after I return this watch, I'm treating you to lunch. What you wanna eat?"

"It's all on you, baby girl."

"Umm, I have a taste for a large Meatlover's."

CHAPTER 34

"Dang, I haven't had any pizza in so long," Quinton said as he and Melanie sat in a booth adjacent from Alonzo and Laila. They were at Pizza Hut and had just received their order.

"Really? You haven't had any *pizza*?"

"That's what I said."

"You sure about that?"

"Yeah."

He took a huge bite of his slice, hardly paying Alonzo any attention.

"Really? If I'm not mistaken you went and got you some *pizza* not too long ago."

"Honey, why didn't you tell me? I had been dying for a slice. What kind did you have?"

"No kind because," he said looking at Alonzo, "I haven't eaten a damn pizza."

"You may not have *ate* it, but you damn sho'll had it."

Laila's eyes grew big and she started choking on her pizza. Then, she started coughing.

"Laila, are you okay?" Melanie asked.

Alonzo patted her on her back. "You alright, babe?"

Quinton tensed as he wiped his mouth with a napkin,

still chewing his food. Laila took a huge sip from her red glass of sweet tea.

"Yes, it just went down the wrong pipe," she cleared her throat, "Now, if you two are finished arguing over meaningless *pizza* that neither of you care about, I would like to continue this date."

"Guys really," Melanie said, "Who cares if Quinton had pizza the other night, as long as he didn't have the whole thing by himself," she patted his stomach, "I want your tux to fit."

"Naw, I got me a slice too," he looked at Quinton while he sipped his tea.

Quinton and Alonzo eyed each other. At that moment, there was rage in Quinton's eyes. He clenched his bottom jaw, his face tensed and the vein at his temple began to pulsate. He looked as if he wanted to jump over the table and take Alonzo out, but he kept his composure.

Melanie and Laila were walking together, arms linked, talking and laughing. Quinton and Alonzo weren't too far behind.

"Man, what the hell was that in there?"

Alonzo shrugged, "You just pissed me off when you told me not to see her anymore."

"Why would you continue seeing her when you know how I feel about her?"

"Q, you can't have your cake and eat it too. You can either be with Melanie or Laila. All I'm trying to do is take Laila out of the equation, so you can be with Melanie."

"Really?"

"You know I went through that before with Alexandra and Gallena. It did not end well…at least not for me, so like I said before, I'm just looking out for you."

"Hmmph. Are you really looking out for me? Or, are you looking out for yourself?" Quinton walked passed him. "We'll continue this tomorrow."

CHAPTER 35

Laila didn't know what was going on between Quinton and Alonzo but it was obvious that it had something to do with her. She tried to get information out of Alonzo when he drove her home but he wouldn't talk about it. He just kissed her on her cheek and drove off. She was glad to finally be at home alone with no distractions until Melanie showed up the next day, bright and early.

They were sitting out on the lanai. "So you're going to have my bridal shower here right?"

"Excuse me?" Laila said as she sipped her orange juice from a wine glass.

"Yes," Melanie explained, "As maid of honor, it is your duty to plan my bridal shower."

"After you've sprung this on me at the last minute?"

"I want it to be nice, but I understand that it may be pressing to order decorations and hors d'oeuvres...ooo, a swan ice sculpture and a white chocolate fountain would be nice."

"And who is going to pay for all of this?"

Melanie giggled, "You, silly."

Laila looked at her in disbelief.

"You can find some items at the low-end retailers, but I

doubt they have any products suitable for a bridal shower, so you may have to run to that party supply place in Atlanta."

"You do realize I have a job."

"Yes, that's why I know my bff can pull this last minute shower off without a glitch. Because you're amazing and very organized. I mean, I don't know where I would be without you, Laila."

Laila rolled her eyes at Melanie's obvious fake sincerity.

"Honestly, Laila," she said sounding like Quinton, "I love you." she hugged Laila, "So can you do this for me? Please," she poked out her bottom lip.

Uh, if I say no, she's going to start crying her infamous crocodile tears.

Laila sighed, "Okay. I'll do it."

"Yah!" Melanie exclaimed.

"But," Laila warned, "I'm only serving finger foods, sandwiches and maybe fruit and cheese trays from Wal-Mart."

Melanie tightened her lips to hold in her comment. She forced herself to say, "Okay, that's fine by me."

"Well okay then,"

"Ooo, I would like for you to scurry up a big crowd for me as my other friends and relatives won't be in until Sunday."

They probably won't be at your wedding either, Laila thought.

"Um, I don't know that many people."

"Oh, you'll figure out something. I don't care who you invite as long as they are not loud, country, obnoxious, ghetto, or Marla Gomillion," she sneered, "And make sure they all bring a gift."

"O-kay, I'll see what I can do."

"Thanks, Laila. You're the best sweetheart," she hugged her.

As she was walking out, she said, "I placed the wedding registry cards on your dining table." Laila's eyes grew wide and she frowned. Melanie had once again already assumed that Laila would agree to her demands.

CHAPTER 36

Quinton and Alonzo were at their local gym. The place was filled with people on ellipticals, treadmills and benches. Alonzo was lifting weights while Quinton stood over him. "I know we talked about it before, but I honestly don't know whether I want to be with Melanie or Laila, and you being with Laila compromises my decision."

Alonzo stopped and looked at him.

"Compromises your decision? Man, are you hearing yourself? You're not some almighty king who gets to pick whichever woman who suits him when he feels like he wants her," he let out a deep breath, "Laila is a grown ass woman. She's not the same girl who was chasing after you in high school."

"Well, why did she sleep with me now then?"

"Keep in mind she slept with me too."

"Just to get back at me. Did she tell you I paid her a visit right before she came to see you that night?"

"A visit? And what did this *visit* involve?"

"We got into this huge argument. I cussed her out, called her all types of names because I thought she was with you. Then, I told her a few more things about me and Melanie that pissed her off."

187

"Really? I would have never done that to her."

Quinton smirked, "Well, after I left, that's when she decided to head your way."

"So, you messed with her head, probably threw it in her face that you were with Melanie, and forced her to run to me?"

"Something like that."

"Ta, whatever man,"

"Do you actually think she would have given you the time of day if I didn't come to her house that night?"

"So it was all a *get back* scheme to her? Is that what you're saying? She wanted revenge on you?"

"Yes," Quinton said, "I know we never argued over a woman, but I have feelings for her, man"

Alonzo sighed, "I can understand that,"

"So what do you say? Will you stop seeing her? I promise I won't ask you to do anything like this again."

Alonzo shook his head and sighed, "Because I value our brotherhood more than any woman, I'll leave her alone."

"Thanks man," they shook hands and did a half-hug.

He exhaled, "Well, I have some serious thinking to do by tomorrow."

Alonzo wiped his face with a white towel. "Seriously, man. You need to stop playing with these women's emotions. You don't even know who you love, do you? Maybe it's neither of them. You ever thought about that?"

Alonzo pulled out his phone as he walked down the hall. Quinton's brows wrinkled. He looked peculiarly, replaying the conversation he had with Marla in his mind.

CHAPTER 37

As Melanie requested, Laila quickly pulled a bridal shower together, thanks to Wal-Mart, Fred's, Dollar General, and Piggly Wiggly. She invited people she saw in the stores and she told Gia to invite everyone at her shop especially the ones that Melanie despised.

Laila was in her kitchen fixing sandwiches while Kecia was outside on the lanai decorating for Melanie's shower. Her phone vibrated on her countertop. She looked at her caller id; it was Alonzo.

"Hey you. I was just thinking about you."

"Yeah me too, uh…" he tried to think of a way to end their fling. He was not used to this; when he left a woman alone, he would just stop calling, but he felt compelled to tell Laila.

"It's hectic over here. We're having a wedding shower for Melanie this evening."

"Laila, listen to me."

"What's wrong?"

He let out a loud sigh, "we can't see each other anymore."

"What? Why not?"

He sighed, "I just ain't feelin' this,"

"Did I do something wrong?"

"Uhh, no that's not it,"

"Then, what is it?"

"Dang, I can't lie to you, Laila. The truth is Quinton doesn't want us to see each other anymore."

"What? That isn't his decision to make."

"He feels the same way you feel about him."

"I don't want-"

"And he doesn't know if he's going to go through with the wedding."

"Really?"

"Let's face it. You're only with me, just to get back at him."

"No I'm not. I-"

"You can lie all you want, but tell me this, if Quinton came to your door right now and asked you to marry him, would you?"

There was a pause.

"I-"

"That's what I thought. So, whatever this was… it's over," he hung up on her.

Kecia and Laila sat down outside and started talking.

"So what are you going to do?"

"What else can I do? I'm in love with Quinton, but if nothing changes, he's marrying Melanie tomorrow."

Kecia shook her head, "Girl, you only think you're in love with Quinton, but you're not. It's all about what you two didn't get in high school. So, what about Alonzo?"

"Well, he makes me feel ways I've never imagined, and whenever I'm with him, I feel so good. But, he broke it off with me. Quinton told him to stop seeing me."

"Huh? Is Quinton y'all damn daddy?" Kecia shook her head again and calmed down, "Well, if Quinton wants you bad enough to tell Alonzo not to see you, then he certainly doesn't need to be marrying Melanie."

"You're right about that."

"So who do you want to be with? Quinton or Alonzo?

"I don't know. I like them both, but one is not about to marry our best friend. I just hate I slept with Quinton."

"You bitch!" They turned around to see Melanie standing in the doorway with tears in her eyes.

"Melanie," Laila's eyes grew wide and her heart began racing.

"Oh shit," Kecia said.

Melanie walked towards Laila.

Kecia got in the middle of them, "Melanie, calm down,"

Melanie ignored her and looked at Laila.

"You backstabbing heartless bitch. I confided in you and you're the bitch that's been sleeping with my fiancé."

"No, it's not what you think."

"Oh, it's not? Then, why do all of Quinton's actions lead to you? Being distant, going through my phone, leaving at all times of the night, his cologne, the tension between him and Alonzo. It was because of you...you, Laila! Explain yourself...talk to me! Find a lie to tell me like you did the other night when I came here, crying to you," she folded her arms.

"No, Melanie. It's not like that."

Melanie cut her eyes at Kecia. "We're fine, Kecia," she said and Kecia stepped aside.

Laila came closer, "Okay, just let me explain," Melanie punched her in the face.

Gia appeared in the doorway with the guests for the party. She didn't notice what was occurring on the patio. "Right through here y'all."

Kecia tried to signal to her to turn around, but it was too late.

"Gia!"

Laila held her face, "You know what I'm tired of being sweet old Laila who's always let you walk all over me. You've always taken from me and taken advantage of me. And on top of that, you're a compulsive liar. You've been trying to get with Quinton since Lord knows when and didn't tell me when you absolutely knew how I felt about him. You didn't even have the audacity to tell me you were with him until you got engaged…until just weeks before the wedding. Then, you flaunted it in my face, asking me to be your maid of honor, just so I could get a front row seat. So bitch, you deserved everything I did to you."

She punched her back and Melanie screamed.

"Now, what the hell is going on out here?" Gia said.

"No, I didn't deserve any of this!"

Melanie lunged at Laila and they started fighting. The women were watching in shock. Most of them were friends of Gia.

"Hey, y'all stop acting a fool. You have guests here," Kecia said, "Gia, help me break them up."

"Uh, uh," Gia shook her head, "Let those bitches fight." She looked in her purse and pulled out some money and held a bill in the air.

"I got fifty on Laila. Anybody want in?"

She looked around at the women, and many of them started pulling out their money. Others were recording the fight on their phones.

"Y'all stop!"

They fell down the steps.

"Ooo," Everything grew quiet.

"Now that had to hurt."

Then, they started rolling around in the grass fighting.

"That's it," Kecia marched down the steps and pulled the girls off one another. When they got up, they were out of breath and tried to lunge at each other again. Melanie picked up her shoe.

"Enough!" Kecia pushed both of them back, "You two need to stop acting like you're still in high school and grow the hell up."

Melanie and Laila never took their eyes off each other.

"It's sad how I always tried to be like you, Little Miss Perfect Goody Two Shoes Laila," Melanie said combining all of Laila's childhood nicknames, "Now, I see you're no better than the bottom of my stiletto."

She looked at the crowd of wordless women gazing back at her. She limped up the stairs.

"The wedding's off."

The crowd opened up for Melanie as she walked onto the patio.

Gia announced, "Okay everyone, show's over. You heard her; the wedding's off. So take y'all asses home and pay me my money at the door."

CHAPTER 38

Quinton heard someone beating on the front door and he rushed to open the door. Melanie appeared wearing a black shirt and blue jeans. Her eyes were bloodshot and teary.

"Hey baby, what's wrong?"

She slapped him.

"What the hell, Melanie?"

She marched over to his mother's couch, grabbed the framed picture of him and Marla from the wall, and smashed it on the floor and glass went everywhere.

"Melanie!"

She looked at him and frowned.

"You slept with Laila?"

His eyes grew wide as he rubbed his face.

"I heard her side, now, I want to hear yours," she folded her arms.

Quinton closed the door.

"What do you need to hear my side for? She told you everything, didn't she?"

"No, I caught her telling Kecia. How could you do this to me? We were going to spend the rest of our lives together, but you slept with my ex-best friend. You threw two years away over some ass you couldn't get in high school."

"Some ass, huh? You've been keeping me from her for years."

"What? No, I haven't."

"You knew I still had feelings for her, that's why you never told her about us. That's why you lied to me and said she was engaged to someone else."

"I admit I stretched the truth, but you-"

"But me? You, Melanie. You try to control everything…our lives together, what I wear… my career."

"Your career?"

"Oh please, girl. You've been dead set against my plans to start my own business for months."

"That's because I thought you were on your way to being a partner."

"A partner? Melanie, you just don't understand how our firm operates,"

"I understand perfectly, I know if you'd make partner in a firm that is already generating millions in revenue we'd be set, but no, you want to go out on a limb and take a huge business risk. What if you fail?"

"I get off my ass, dust myself off, and rise again,"

She shook her head.

"See that's exactly your problem, you want to wear the pants and control every detail of our lives. You wouldn't even let me design any of our invitations, programs, displays, nothing. Then, you wanted expensive platters and dishes when I'm fine with some damn clear plastic plates from Wal-Mart or *low-end retailers* as you call the places our families utilized to fulfill our needs or have you've forgotten where you come from?"

"I know exactly where I come from."

"Yeah, right. You even tried to control what pictures my mom put up in her house." He gestured towards the shattered picture.

"Well, I don't want to be looking at you and Marla

whenever I come over with *my* husband," she said in a fast, informal tone without her proper accent.

Quinton shook his head. "You have to learn there's some things in life you can't control."

"Like sleeping with my best friend, the bitch everyone claims I've always controlled."

"Well, it's true. You're worse than Genevieve! You're controlling and you want what everyone else has or what they aspire to have. You try your best to get it with no regard for anyone else's feelings. Maybe my indiscretion with Laila is your karma."

Her mouth dropped. "Don't you dare put this on me… don't you dare blame me for your infidelity," she let out a scream of frustration, "No, I didn't go through all of this trouble to be with you for nothing."

"What trouble did you go through, Melanie?"

"I guess I should tell you now. We didn't meet by coincidence at the apartment. I set the whole thing up."

"You did what?" he asked, "How?"

"You've been my Facebook friend for five years now. I bet you didn't even know that. You invited everyone in your friend's list to a party at your apartment, so I wrote down your address and since my lease was up, I moved there. It was a smart move since it was closer to my job. So, I jogged by your building each day after work until we finally bumped into each other."

"That's…that's crazy,"

"Oh it is? I'll tell you what's crazy. I've secretly wanted you since we were in junior high before Laila and I even became friends. But, you never noticed me; you would look right through me in class and in the halls. Then, in high school, you noticed Laila and that's when you finally started talking to me and listening to what I had to say."

He shook his head.

"So, when the opportunity to be with you without Laila encompassing your mind-when *that* opportunity presented itself- I took it, so excuse me for wanting to be with you *just* that much, Quinton."

He placed his hands behind his head and walked around.

"You are unbelievable, man,"

There was silence.

"Do you love her?"

"What?"

"You heard me, do you love her?"

"Melanie-"

"Cuz if you don't, I- I can forgive you. I can – I can make us work somehow," she exhaled and began to speak with her proper accent again, "I love you for better or worse, Quinton. We can get through this. We can still have the wedding tomorrow."

"Melanie, are you hearing yourself? I slept with your...your...your sister."

"Well, if she means nothing to you, I will forgive you if, in turn, you forgive me for my previous and final attempts to control you." she said, "So what is it going to be? Her or me?"

Quinton sighed, "I- I don't know,"

"You don't know now?" she fumed, "Well, when you make up your mind, you know where to find me." She made her way out of the door and slammed it behind her.

CHAPTER 39

"Boy, what have you gotten yourself into now?"

"How did you hear?"

"I was at the beauty salon getting my hair styled when they told me."

"I'm sorry, Mom."

She sighed and sat beside him. "So you were seeing the bride *and* her maid of honor? What were you thinking?"

Quinton shrugged. "I guess I wasn't thinking."

She let out a deep breath and shook her head. "I've been worried since that night you disappeared at the engagement party, and I had a bad feeling once I saw that girl standing beside Melanie at the rehearsal. I never formally met her when you were kids, but when we saw her in town, I saw the way you two looked at each other. And those pictures that you still have in that drawer yields a thousand emotions that I can never imagine feeling and you two were just children. There's no telling how deep it runs now that you're grown. Do you think it's love?"

"I don't know. I do feel for her, but I'm just confused right now, Momma."

"Well, this is a big mess you've made. If you had these feelings for her, then why did you get involved with her girlfriend?"

He exhaled. "I never intended to. Melanie was just a familiar face in a different state. We ended up living at the same apartment complex, so we started hanging out and I would always ask about Laila. Then, after a while, I stopped asking and started to develop feelings for Melanie."

She sighed, "Quinton, listen to me good. Who do you really love? Who completes you? Who is the woman you wake up thinking about every morning? Who makes you happy? Who can you picture spending the rest of your life with? If you can answer those questions, then that is the woman you need to marry," she got up, "Now, I'm about to roll my hair in case there is a wedding tomorrow."

Quinton picked up his phone and called Taaz.

"Come on, Taaz. Pick up, man." No answer.

***

At the casino, Kecia was sitting at the bar twirling a straw around in a full glass of Vodka. Before she got with Leonard, she always loved to come to the casino. It was only in the next town about 25 miles away. She would always come on Saturday nights and sit at the bar because they played R&B songs from artists like Usher, Beyoncé, Monica, and Anthony Hamilton.

"Damn girl, you're everywhere I go."

"Hey Taaz," she looked up as he sat beside her.

"I heard about the wedding. That's messed up."

"Yes, it is."

"But that ain't what's bothering you, is it?"

"Nope, I discovered my boyfriend is actually cheating on me."

"Damn, now that's really messed up."

She sighed, "My friends tried to warn me, and the signs were constantly knocking me in the face, but I didn't take heed to any of it."

"Aw, don't beat yourself down for it. It happens to the best of us."

"You've been cheated on?"

"Yep, Kanesha Gill."

"Oh yea, I heard about that."

"Umm huh, but I'm over her," he said, "so how did you find out?"

She sighed once again.

"He was supposed to be on a business trip, but when I visited his job, his fellow employee told me he was on vacation. He claimed he couldn't take a vacation this year because he didn't reach a quota. You know this fool even made a printout just to show me how many cars he was supposed to sell just to be able to take one."

"Damn, if I would have to do all of that, it wouldn't be worth it."

She exhaled.

"So what are you going to do?" he looked at her.

"There's nothing I can do, but kick him to the curb when he gets back. I wish I could do it right now, but I can't contact him. He called me one time and told me he dropped his cell phone in the toilet, and even if he bought a new phone it would be bad reception in the area he's in. Nothing but lies."

"He probably just didn't want to be bothered."

"Yeah, he didn't want me to interrupt a second of his vacation in Montego Bay."

"Jamaica?"

She nodded and said with a Jamaican accent, "Jamaica, mon."

"Damn, he all the way out there? I bet you he ain't even take you anywhere like that," he said. Kecia shook her head, "Yeah, just let that go."

"So? What about you? Any special person in your life right now?"

"Naw, they all say the same thing, *I* don't take life seriously... I don't care what anyone says; I'm not about to

200

walk around with a stick in my ass. The way I see it … if they can't take time out to laugh, then *they're* taking life too seriously."

"Uh huh," she raised her glass, "Here's to the single life."

"I heard that."

They clanged glasses and looked at each other while they drank. Just then, her favorite song flooded the lounge. He was staring at her. He asked her to dance. She refused, but he got up and held out his hand. She reluctantly accepted. Soon, they were on the dance floor, dancing with almost a foot of space between the two. She wouldn't look him in the eyes. He twirled her around and pulled her close.

"I won't bite, Kecia. I promise."

She glanced at him and pursed her lips. They were dancing slower than the tempo. She started looking around the casino lounge at the other couples. He held her chin and gently turned her face to him. She finally looked him in the eye and he placed his forehead on hers. She soon became lost in his eyes and wrapped her arms around him.

"Kecia, you are beautiful, girl. You've always been beautiful exactly how you are," she pictured him entering her classroom, and him pressing against her when they were in high school. Kecia just stared at him. He gently kissed her and when he slowly pulled away, she kept staring at his lips and came forward and kissed him. Then, the two began making out then she broke away.

"Taaz, I – I – I have to go."

She attempted to walk away, but he held her hand.

"No, I won't let go, Kecia. I ran away from this a long time ago. I fought it, you fought it. Let's just figure out what this is that's always been between us. I ain't running no more Kecia, so don't you run away from me. Be with me, right here…right now."

***

Quinton was in his room. He had pulled out his sketch pad and made a list of likes and dislikes in Melanie and Laila. He was lost; as he stared at his list, he thought if he could only get a sign to show which woman to pick, which woman he was supposed to spend the rest of his life with.

His phone buzzed, interrupting his thoughts. He stared at the number; it had a Tennessee area code. He silently hoped it wasn't one of his exes.

"Hello?"

"Quinton. I'm glad you're still up."

"Hearst?"

"Yes, is this a convenient time for you to talk?"

"Oh umm…yes."

"So uh…how is everything coming along? The big day is tomorrow, right?"

"Yes, just making some last minute decisions," he sighed, "Decisions…that's all I have to make."

"Well, speaking of which, that's the reason I called. I know you're focusing on your wedding, but I bet your career isn't too far from your mind…I uh…"

Quinton was surprised; He had never heard his boss being at a loss of words.

"I know you feel let down by our company. You're not sure whether you want to come back to us, or take your talent elsewhere, or you may even be thinking of spreading your wings and opening a smaller, more specialized firm. You have all of these options, but we really don't want to lose you, Quinton. You're a valuable part of our team which is why I would like to offer you a promotion."

"Whoa...are you serious? A promotion?"

"Yes, I would like you to be our new Creative Director of Marketing," Quinton said trying to let it sink in.

"Whoa, what happened to Phil?"

"Oh, he's transferring to one of our older firms in Seattle to be closer to his daughter and her family."

"Well, Does Mitchell know about this?"

"Actually, he's not my partner anymore. He handed the reigns over to his son, Allen and I've been knowing him since he was a kid. In fact, I taught him everything he knows and well Yale too. You're gonna love him. He's smart, creative, and even has a gym membership," he joked and Quinton forced a chuckle.

"Creative Director of Marketing."

"Has a nice ring to it, doesn't it? You take your time, even take a nice honeymoon. The job will be waiting for you when you get back. You'll have Phil's huge office and we'll discuss your impressive pay raise and benefits when you come back to the office. Or, we can discuss it now, if you'd like."

"Oh no, that's fine. We'll discuss it in further detail later this week."

"Oh okay. Congratulations, Quinton. I know you're going to make that lovely lady one happy bride," he said. "Oh, and I understand that offering you a promotion doesn't mean you'll decide to stay with us, but I hope you will carefully consider the offer."

"I will let you know soon."

"Okay, oh and Quinton, when you're making a decision, the heart and mind never agrees. It's never in your best interest to follow what the mind tells you; follow your heart. That's what I always do. My heart told me to find some way to get rid of Mitchell and I did; my heart told me to fight to get you in that Director position and that's what I'm currently trying to do. So, do what's in your heart. Either way, we wish you the best."

CHAPTER 40

"… I love you with all of my heart. You are the only person I want. Please call me. Love, Laila."

She hung up the phone, hoping that at least one of her voicemail messages would reach him before it's too late. She had finally found the one, and she was hoping to finally have her happy ending. She paced for a while, holding onto her phone, but a call never came.

She walked slowly to her bedroom and into her bathroom. She turned on her stereo and decided to play her favorite Adele song on repeat. She looked at the clock and it was 12:02 once again. She decided to soak all of her problems away in her garden tub.

Soon, Laila was lying in a bath of thoughts. Bubbles of despair covered her, and poured over the sides of the tub. She immersed herself beneath the bubbles into the water hoping to drown away all of her sins. Then, she came back up for air. She finally took a sip of the champagne that so desperately needed her attention on the side of the tub. She closed her eyes as the alcohol went down.

Was being bad worth it? Did I just ruin my reputation for nothing?

She had always been known and respected for being safe, generous, innocent, and virtuous. *Virtuous. Why did everyone put me on a pedestal? Like I could do no wrong. I'm human like everyone else, but no matter what, others get what they want and I don't.*

The gossip of Laila's sexscapades and the fight spread through town like wildfire. She wondered what people thought of her now. Where they calling her a whore? A derogatory term she never thought would be associated with her. She literally tarnished her reputation after a week. She slept with two men in one week, two best friends, an engaged man, her best friend's fiancé.

What was I thinking? Now, Quinton is supposed to be making a decision, he needs to…

Her doorbell interrupted her thoughts.

"Someone's finally using my doorbell," she quickly got out of the tub and dried off. She rushed into her room and threw on her black robe. The doorbell sounded again all throughout the house. She hurried down the hall, through the living room, and to the door. She looked out of the window to make sure it wasn't Melanie and then she opened the door. To her surprise, it was Quinton.

He looked her directly in the eye.

"Hey, we have to talk."

"Yes we do."

She let him in and closed the door behind him.

CHAPTER 41

The next morning, Kecia awoke in her bed. She stretched and turned over.

"Umm, last night was amazing."

"It sure was."

Taaz turned over towards her. They looked at each other and start screaming.

"Did we really?"

He looked under the covers.

"Oh yes we did."

"Do you remember anything?"

"I ain't even gon' lie. I do."

"Oh, it's all coming back to me," she put her hand to her head and started to pant, "Every mind blowing detail. I just can't believe it….me and you?"

They heard someone unlocking Kecia's front door. Her eyes grew wide.

"Ooo, that's Leonard. What do we do?"

Leonard appeared in the doorway holding a duffle bag with his coat on top in one hand and a bouquet of roses in the other. He also had a newspaper tucked under his arm. His eyes grew wide as he discovered Kecia and Taaz in bed kissing. He dropped his duffle bag.

"Oh darling. I didn't expect you to come back so soon. Did you enjoy your vacation?"

"How- how? Kecia, how could you do this to me?"

"You had all of this coming to you. You've been cheating on me and attacking my self-esteem for months, so I'm through with you. And as you can clearly see, I've already moved on to something bigger and hell of a lot better."

"You see, I appreciate all of her curves and you best believe I took my time to explore every single one."

"Shut the hell up, you street thug."

"Man, who you think you talking to?"

Kecia held Taaz's arm.

"Leonard, it's over, so just get out and don't even bother coming back."

"Not before I kick both of your asses."

He came towards them. Taaz jumped out of the bed like a jet.

"Man, I wish you would."

Just as Taaz was about to reach him, Leonard let out a high-pitched scream, threw down the roses and newspaper, and quickly grabbed his duffel bag. He ran out of the apartment and slammed the door behind him. Taaz looked down the hall, laughed, and shook his head, "Punk ass," then, he picked up the roses and walked back to Kecia's queen-sized bed.

"I think these belong to you. From me to you."

He handed her the roses and she smelled them.

"Oh how thoughtful," she said sarcastically and smiled.

"You know what? We're not drunk, so we have complete control of our actions. You wanna-"

"Oh hell yes."

She threw the roses on the floor, and Taaz jumped back in bed and pulled the covers over them.

"Wait," he heard his phone buzz. He reached down on

the floor, picked up his jeans, and pulled out his phone. "Dang, somebody been blowin' me up."

She laid back and started rubbing his arm.

"The wedding's back on."

"Really?"

"Quinton wants us to meet him in 20 minutes."

"Oh. Well, that gives us more than enough time."

She grabbed him and started kissing him.

"Damn, girl. You don't know what you do to me."

"Naw, you don't know what I'm about to do to you."

He raised his brows and Kecia pulled the sheets over their heads.

CHAPTER 42

The church was filled with guests, every pew filled with disapproving, shocked, and disturbed relatives, friends, and inquisitive people. The church was adorned beautifully with red and white decor. Red was the signifying color of love, and in opposition, betrayal, lust, and sin. Many people were smiling happily, others were confused, and most of them shook their heads in disdain. They were mainly at the church to see if there was going to be any drama like objections and more fights. Maybe they wanted to see if someone was going to back out of this whole *sham*. A cameraman stood against the wall, preparing to record this day for everyone to relive over and over again.

Quinton was smiling from ear to ear and looked relieved and very much in love. He seemed satisfied with his choice.

"I'm glad you said yes," he looked at her.

"Are you two ready?" Pastor Thomas asked.

"Oh yes we are," Quinton said. He lifted up the veil and revealed Marla Gomillion.

Pastor Thomas proceeded with the wedding ceremony. Gia and Kecia were sitting in the congregation on the bride's side, shaking their heads. Marla looked at the front pew and her mother was smiling back at her with tears in her eyes.

"Uh, uh, uh," Gia shook her head.

"Now, this is a damn shame," Kecia said.

Taaz was staring at Kecia, smiling at her. She looked over at him. She smiled back and admired her new man dressed in his tux, never taking her eyes off him. Gia observed them.

"Uhhh huh," she pursed her lips.

After the wedding, Alonzo was standing in the church lobby. The front doors of the church were propped open. People were passing by him on their way to the reception. Some spoke, some nodded. A beautiful woman approached him.

"Hi, I don't usually do this, but I was admiring you all throughout the ceremony. Actually, I couldn't stop looking at you. I was wondering maybe we could go out sometimes."

Alonzo sighed.

"You're very attractive and I can't believe I'm saying this, but I'm just not up to dating anyone right now."

"Did I come on too strong?"

"No, no. It's not you."

She shrugged. "Well, you can't blame a girl for trying. If you change your mind, Natilee Gray, look me up on Facebook," she walked down the stairs as David rushed up. He stopped in his tracks and stared at her for a moment.

He finally reached Alonzo and handed him a phone.

"It took you long enough."

"I thought you had left it in the Mercedes, but it was stuck between your seat and the console."

"Well, I guess I can turn it back on now since everything's over," he checked his phone.

"Damn, 10 messages."

"It's probably Laila trying to get with you now that Quinton has picked Marla."

"Probably so and I come second to no man."

"I heard that. Ooo, I have to piss."

He rushed to the bathroom while Alonzo checked his voicemail. The first message was from Alonzo's mother, Alice.

"Hey baby, this is Mom. Tell Quinton, I'm sorry but I won't be able to make it to the wedding. Call me when you get this message. I love you baby. Bye."

End of message. Message two.

"Hey this is Melanie. I was wondering if-"

Alonzo frowned and pressed a button on his phone.

Message has been deleted. Message three.

"Dear Alonzo, you didn't give me a chance to answer you. There's no way I would pick Quinton over you. . ."

"Oh, you're saying that now."

"I was just caught up in an old high school crush. I don't love him. I never did, and I know that now. Alonzo, I want to be with you, not him. You're all I think about, and it's hurting me that we can't be together because you are who I want without a doubt in my mind. You have always been my Romeo and I, your Juliet. I know I fought my feelings for you back then, but never again. Please just talk to me. Sincerely yours, Laila."

Alonzo smirked. He decided to delete the rest of his messages. Then, he checked his text messages. The first name that his eyes went to was Laila. He selected the message. It read, *but I want you. Please listen to my voicemail message.* He checked the date and time. She had sent the message on April 21st at 8:45pm.

"What?"

He looked in sudden shock. He just stared at the phone for a moment, then slowly let his hand, still firmly grasping his phone, fall to his side. He looked as if he was in a trance.

"So she sent me a love letter through my voicemail yesterday before Quinton even knew who he wanted to be with," he said, then repeated, "Yesterday."

"Dang, I feel better. I didn't know I was holding all of that in. You're ready to go to the reception?"

"Um …Ah, tell Quinton I'll catch him when he gets back from the honeymoon. I have something I need to do."

"Are you serious?"

Alonzo rushed down the steps.

"Ah, how am I going to get there? I rode with you. Ah!"

CHAPTER 43

Quinton came to see me last night to tell me he was in love, not lust, but in love with Marla. It shocked me at first, but I'm happy for him. Then, I told him I wanted to be with Alonzo, but he wouldn't return my calls after I poured my heart out to him in a voicemail.

Quinton apologized for forbidding Alonzo to see me, and asked me if I wanted him to talk to Alonzo. I didn't, knowing that from now on, the only thing that can be between Quinton and I is a simple handshake. Yes, in a surprising turn of events, Quinton chose Marla and I'm happy for them. His heart had always been with her. I'm just glad he finally admitted it to himself. I sincerely hope that, through this whole ordeal, they find peace and happiness in their marriage.

Laila was sitting at the bar, writing in her journal. Melanie entered and sat on the far right side. A couple came in, dressed in their Sunday's best. They had Quinton's freshly designed wedding program with a colored picture of him and Marla on the front. They both looked at Melanie, then Laila. The woman whispered in the man's ear and he laughed hysterically. They got up, but left the program on the bar.

Melanie was drinking a tall mug of beer. She got up

and sat in their spot so she could take a look at her ex-fiancé's program that he had designed at the last minute. The two glanced at each other while Melanie took a huge gulp of beer and stared at their picture.

"Cosmopolitan, please," Laila said to the bartender as she placed her pen in her journal and sat it down on the bar stool next to her.

"After all of that, Quinton didn't want you or me. Don't we look like some damn fools?" Melanie started laughing and Laila shook her head.

"When we were fighting, he probably was with that bitch," she pointed at the program, laughing again. Melanie got up and tried to compose herself, then sat beside Laila.

"Ah, give me a bottle of water," she told the bartender, then turned to Laila, "I thought about it long and hard and talked to God. After some drinks, I finally started to listen, and I know He's gonna get me for that in the morning. But do you know what He told me?"

"What?"

"He told me, you're no better yourself. Then I thought about it. If the shoe was on the other foot, and you ended up with my high school sweetheart, Avery King."

"Yeah, you loved Avery. He worsh-"

"And if you two were getting married, I probably would have slept with him too."

"You would have."

"I'm sorry. I shouldn't have looked his way. I shouldn't have kept you two from communicating …The list just goes on, but I'm truly sorry for all of it."

"And I'm sorry for being with him behind your back, lying to you, and ruining your wedding."

"Well, I'm glad he showed his true colors before I got myself into marriage for it to end in a messy divorce," Melanie sighed, "So are we friends again?"

"We still have some issues to work out, but yeah," she smiled and they hugged each other.

"I trust this won't happen again when I start back

dating."

"You have my word."

"Good because I'm in town for good."

"Really?"

A guy approached them.

"Hi, you're Melanie, right?"

"Yes I am and you are?"

"Carmelo Hudson, I was two years behind you in high school."

"Oh, I thought you looked familiar."

"I heard what happened. Quinton must be a damn fool letting a beautiful woman like you go. I know I was a fool in high school when I couldn't build up the nerve to ask you out."

She was blushing.

"I was wondering if we could sit at a table and catch up."

"Of course we can."

He took her hand and helped her get off the stool. She winked at Laila and followed him to a table. She watched a group of college kids as they came in. She sipped her drink as Alonzo, still wearing his tuxedo, entered.

"Hey, I missed you."

She put her drink down. He kissed her on the cheek and held her hands.

"Laila, I don't care what anyone says or how they feel about you. All I know is that I want to be with you and only you. Every woman I've encountered pales in comparison to you. You complete me," he pulled her to her feet as Kecia and Gia entered.

Gia was busy talking to Kecia about Quinton, "Girl, I heard he went out and bought her a brand new car with On-star service."

They stopped in their tracks as Alonzo got down on one knee, reached in his pocket, and pulled out a black box. Laila's eyes grew wide.

She gasped. "What? No, Alonzo you can't be serious."

"But I am serious, baby."

"It's too soon. You're just caught up in the whole wedding excitement."

This is a joke. He's just pulling my leg. Any minute now he's going to burst out laughing and say, Sike!

"Will you marry me?"

"Huh?"

Am I hearing the right words? This isn't a practical joke. Alonzo Davis actually wants to marry me? After what I've done?

Melanie called. "Girl, answer him."

Kecia and Gia quickly turned and looked in her direction.

"Carmelo?" They both said.

"Well, she's over Quinton," Kecia said.

"Just like Melanie to dust herself off and jump right onto the next one."

Laila was still in shock.

"What did you ask me?"

He opened the ring box.

"Will you marry me?"

"Wha-Where did you get this?"

"It was my grandmother's. She gave it to me after my grandfather passed a few years ago. She told me to save it for the right woman. So?" he raised the box up closer to her.

She shook her head, "Alonzo, we have to date for a while…you know… take it slow. We just can't jump into something."

"Laila, I'm not trying to rush you into something. We can be engaged for a year or even get married five years from now. I'll wait. During that time, if you feel I am not the one, we can go our separate ways. But, Laila, I feel you are *my* one. You remember when I told you I wanted to reassess my life?"

She swallowed hard and nodded.

"Well, my mind kept leading me to you. I thought of all I've experienced and I didn't expect it but I started dreaming about you and I didn't know why. I just wanted to see you and see if I'll still be attracted to you and I was. In fact, it is so much stronger and you've become such a beautiful woman," he took a deep breath and licked his lips, "Laila, we can date for however long you'd like, but I just want you to know- right here, right now- I want you to be my wife before anyone who fits your preconceived idea of the perfect man enters your life and whisks you away from me…I- I just can't risk that. I want to wake up each day and see your beautiful face cuz you are the perfect woman for me… I had always been scared since I was a kid to put my heart out there for any woman, so I would hurt them before they get a chance to hurt me," he held her face and caressed her cheek, "but Laila, you are the first and only woman that I would not hurt. I've always wanted to protect you and I want to protect you, provide for you, and love you for the rest of my life."

He paused. "We have so much in common on both a personal and professional level. You make me laugh with your quirkiness and that sassy ass attitude. You evoke every emotion in my body. Emotions I never thought I could feel," he held both her hands, "The bible says…"

"How you gon' quote the bible in a bar?"

Alonzo cut his eyes at Gia.

"I'm just saying," Gia said, "Proceed."

He looked at Laila, "The bible says your words have power and freshman year, I called you my wife every day for exactly one hundred and eighty-one days. I was speaking us into existence. I was speaking our future, so Laila, let's fulfill this prophecy, be my wife."

Tears came to her eyes. She nodded her head. Everyone clapped while he put the ring on her finger.

"A perfect fit."

He picked her up and kissed her.

Her girls came up.

"See, your man came and found you," Kecia embraced her, "Congratulations."

"Yeah, everybody ain't able to do dirt and come out on top in the end."

Kecia hit her. "Quit hating."

Gia smiled. "Congratulations girl." She said as she hugged Laila.

Melanie came up. "After all of the mess you put me through, I know I'm going to be your maid of honor."

"Nuh uh, I'm gonna be the maid of honor," Gia said.

"No, you bitches better step back… I am," Kecia said.

"Uh oh," Alonzo said as he laughed to himself.

"We'll think about that when the time comes."

"Well, we're gonna lock up Melanie to keep her away from Alonzo 'cuz I don't want to see a part two of this," Gia said.

The ladies laughed.

"Hey, he's my cousin."

"Whateva."

"Come here you," Alonzo said as he pulled Laila against him and planted a long passionate kiss on her.

ACKNOWLEDGEMENTS

I would like to first give God all the glory, honor, and praise. I tried to do things my way for years and came to a standstill each time. Once I surrendered to God, things began to fall in place; the right people entered my life and doors began to open. Though I face many challenges, God has given me the strength to embrace each one, endure, press forward, and conquer all. And, now I confidently declare, "I can do all things through Christ which strengthens me."

I would like to thank two special little men in my life. Sons, you are my greatest gifts from God. I'm thankful to spend each day with you and watch you grow and develop your talents. You inspire me and push me even when I feel like giving up at times. I get back up and try again because I want the best for you. I want to be an example to you and show you that you can be anything you want to be whether it's a doctor, artist, animator, basketball player, or football player. I'm here to encourage you just as you've been encouraging me and praying for me to be an author. Mommy loves you!

A huge thank you to my mother, father, siblings and the rest of the family including my church family. Friends, colleagues, and family, I truly appreciate your support, advice, reality checks, and pep talks. You have all made sacrifices for me and words cannot express how honored I am to have each and every one of you in my life. Much love to you all.

I would also like to acknowledge three special angels. My grandmother, Irene Lyle, it's been over 15 years and I still love you with all of my heart. Thank you for encouraging me to read God's Word. My children's paternal grandparents, Andrew "Moto" and Virginia Leflore, thank you for treating me as your own and inspiring me to step out in faith. Your love and words of encouragement still remain in my heart.

Last but not least, thank you for purchasing this book and taking the time to explore the world of these colorful characters. I hope you enjoyed it and I look forward to sharing more stories with you soon!

ABOUT THE AUTHOR

Dominique Lewis currently works as a professional copywriter. She received a bachelor's degree in Interdisciplinary Studies from Mississippi State University. She is a mother of two and resides in MS. In her spare time, Dominique likes to sing and indulge in food, music, fashion, and entertainment. She is also an active member of Life in Christ Ministries.

Connect with me online!
Follow @dominiquenlewis on Instagram
or Like my page on Facebook to get the latest info on upcoming releases:
https://www.facebook.com/dominiquenicolelewis/